BE MY GAME CHANGER

ANDREA ROUSSE

To Krista,
It's not where you go. It's who you meet along the way.
—The Wizard of Oz
I'm forever grateful to have crossed paths with you on this journey
and am truly blessed to call you a friend!

1

AVERY

"About time."

"Miss me that much?" Bodie steps into my apartment with that beaming face I've been waiting for all morning. Wasting no time, he makes himself at home, heading into the kitchen to pour a glass of water.

"Nope, but I'm ready to get this shopping trip over with." I grab my purse, slinging it over my shoulder. I attempt to sound frustrated, but my lips automatically curl into a smile as my best friend turns his heart-melting grin back to me.

"You're a girl, aren't you supposed to love shopping? Besides, I need someone to help me not look like a fool."

"That boat sailed many years ago." I smirk as I throw the jab. I don't know who he thinks he's fooling, we both know he couldn't care less about making an ass of himself. In fact, it's his calling card. Bodie usually goes out of his way to act foolish, forever desiring to be the center of attention. While I on the other hand, prefer to hang out in the background, unnoticed. It's one of the many reasons our lifelong friendship has thrived.

"Touché. But I have to look decent for my brother's

engagement party, and my only other option is shopping with Mom. You know how she tries to set me up with any single female in sight." He gives me a fearful look as I raise my eyebrows, not actually considering making him shop with her, but it's fun to watch the panic as it plays out in his mind. "Please, Avery. Don't bail on me. Think of all the single retail workers you'll be saving."

"Oh, stop being such a baby. Your mom just wants you to settle down already. Plus, I have the entire day free. I even stayed up late last night to get papers graded so I could devote my day to helping you, because for some reason, I actually want to spend the day with my best friend who hasn't been around much lately."

"Yeah. The office has been keeping me busy, and I really want to spend time with my BFF too." He pauses, and I feel it coming.

I prop my hand on my hip and look to him. "But?"

"No *but*, just ... a slight alteration on today's itinerary," he says hesitantly as he shrugs.

"What 'alteration'? I thought today was your only free day for party attire shopping?"

"It is. But"—I nod at the word I knew was coming—"my dad gave me tickets for the ball game today."

I'm not even mad because I know how much he and his entire family love baseball. "Okay. Well, I guess shopping will have to wait. Have fun at the game with your dad."

"Oh no, my dad can't go. He got the tickets for us because he knew we planned to hang out today. It's an afternoon game, so I figure we can hit the shops afterwards."

"Bodie, really? As if shopping wasn't bad enough, now you want me to sit through a baseball game beforehand?"

"We don't have to stay for the entire game. I really just want to see the first few innings."

"Is that your selling point? Because I'm not buying that

you want me to schlep to the stadium just to see *part* of the game."

"No really. Carter Barlowe is pitching, and I *gotta* see how it goes—along with all of Canaan Falls."

"O-kay …" My eyes roll as the solution seems simple. "DVR it."

"It's not the same. I need the atmosphere if I'm going to be the envy of the podcast world."

More like the envy of the uber-amateur, bro'd out Talking Sports, Taking Stats sports-nerds podcast world he and his brothers care about so much. "Fine. I'll meet you after you watch your atmospheric pitcher."

"No, it's the first time he's pitching for the Coyotes," he informs me emphatically, like this should be common knowledge. "Avery, don't you watch the news or anything? Even non-sports people know all about him. His dad is Cash Barlowe. Won the Coyotes the pennant three years in a row."

"Yes, Cash rings a bell." Only because Bodie and all the boys constantly compare every Coyote player to him.

"Well, his son is on track to be as great of a player, if not better, but an injury sidelined him. This is his first regular-season game back since his Tommy John surgery last year, and it's going to set the tone for the rest of his season."

"Okay."

"It's a big deal, Avery. I really want to be there, *and* I really want to hang out. So, just come with me, and we'll watch him pitch then we'll leave from there to go shopping. We'll beat the traffic if we leave early, anyways."

"Bodie, really. I'll meet you afterwards. I'm sure one of your brothers would love to go instead."

"Exactly. And that's why they're not invited."

"How are y'all so competitive with something as simple as who gets to see Baby Cash throw a damn ball?"

"It's all in love. Tough love, but still love."

Rolling my eyes, I look down at my jean shorts and white linen button-down. "I wasn't prepared for a baseball game." Not that I'd even know what the proper attire would be.

"You look beautiful, Avery. I know it's not your favorite way to spend the day, but I promise next time I'll do something you want to do that bores me to death."

"Yeah, sure." I grab the paperback I'd been reading while waiting on him and tuck it into my bag. "I have a cure for your boring pursuit."

"That's what I'll do. I'll sit and read with you for an entire day. It sounds utterly horrendous." He grabs my bag and holds it up. "I brought Mom's clear bag for you to use."

"You really did plan ahead with the assumption I'd say yes."

"Why wouldn't I? I knew my charm would wear you down eventually. Although, I thought it'd take a little more convincing." He gives me a cocky smirk that would make any other girl melt, but for me, it's like looking at my annoying brother who knows he's going to get his way.

"We're not there yet." I grab my bag from him and head out the door. I might be planning to go along for the game, but that won't stop me from complaining the entire way. Though I'm excited to spend the day with him, why'd he go and pick two of my least favorite activities? Baseball and shopping, bleh.

CARTER

"You ready to go?" Coach Dundee asks. His stance widens, arms folding over his chest as he tilts his head slightly to the right. It's my pitching coach's typical posture when he's evaluating me, and I've seen it too many times over the last few weeks.

"Yep, all warmed up," I say, turning my attention to the field. From the bullpen, I can see the stadium is packed. That's never bothered me before, and I can't let it now.

"Warmed up and ready are two different things," Dundee says as I turn my attention back to him.

"My arm's good, Coach. All those minor league games you had me pitch in should've showed you that."

"Your arm is the least of my worries today. Stepping on the same mound as your father is your biggest challenge today. Combine that with all the other bullshit …"

Damn. I've kept my feelings for my piece of shit father well hidden from everyone except the man assessing me right now. And he sees right through me. "I got it. I have nothing to prove to him or his ancient fan club."

Dundee gives me an encouraging pat on the shoulder.

"The only person you have to convince today is yourself." He nods towards the field. "Need another rundown of the lineup?"

"Nope. I got it." I point to my temple. I've memorized the batting order and every stat possible on each hitter. Knowing my opponent is the best way I can prepare myself, so that's what I've always done. I probably know their stats better than they do.

"Alrighty. Let's get out there with our team." He motions towards the dugout.

Our team. Never thought I'd be donning the royal-blue uniform or referring to the Coyotes as "my" team. But here I am, a year after being cut loose from the Evergreens, the tools who released me two months after my surgery. *But I came back, you bastards.* Clenching my fist, I extend my arm, remembering the tightness, recalling the range of motion I'd lost, and compare it to how I feel now—confident, at the top of my game, best shape of my life. Now it's time to prove it.

Stepping out of the bullpen, my mind clicks into game mode as I join my teammates. After the national anthem and team introductions, it's finally time to step on the mound. I attempt to keep emotion off my face, but it's everything. No matter that it's the mound my father stood on, it's home, and there were times I thought I'd never be here again. But I was hell-bent on a homecoming, and thankfully my body agreed.

When the first batter steps up, I nod to my catcher, Lynch, accepting his pitch call. Sliders aren't the ones I'm known for, but it's the best one to use against the player I'm up against at the moment. And sure enough, three pitches later, I send his ass back to the bench as the second batter makes his way into the box.

Lynch won't call a splitter, the one I'm most well-known for delivering with perfection every time. The hitter's expecting a splitter, but I know how to work that to my advantage, and Lynch is with me when he calls for a sinker. I nod and deliver with more side spin than the batter expected. When I told Dundee I knew these players, I meant it.

Strike one.

I throw a changeup on the second toss, and he fouls it away before I deliver a clean strike with the third throw.

Yes. I knew I was back, but this proves it. Glancing around the stadium, I absorb the sea of blue, fans on their feet cheering me on—not my father, *me*. And I wrap up the top of the first after three more pitches, striking out the third batter. *One-two-three inning. Let's go.*

Making my way off the field, I take in the enthusiasm of the crowd around me and the announcer's booming voice. Damn, I missed this. I scan the stadium rows in front of me, seeing fans on their feet. Clapping, cheering, whistling. Well, all except one. Bafflingly, a brunette sits in the first row behind the dugout, catching my attention only because hers is focused on the book she holds, ass firmly planted in her seat, completely oblivious to the chaos and shouting around her.

Squinting and shaking my head, I step down into the dugout, and plop onto the hard bench. One inning down, hopefully six or seven more tonight, and many additional games to go. A few of my teammates give me an encouraging word as they pass, pounding my fist, but Dundee doesn't bypass me and instead parks his ass on the bench next to me.

"How's the arm?"

"No complaints."

"Well, I have one," Dundee stands and leans over. "That ego of yours is gonna get bigger." His annoyance contradicts the supportive slap he gives my knee as he walks away. He has faith in me and my abilities, but he also knows our bodies don't always follow through.

I spend the bottom of the inning mentally reviewing Dundee's analysis of the Hawks lineup and strategizing with Lynch on one particular hitter, then I'm back on the mound. Three batters up, three batters struck out. Boom. A hitless inning. *Doing my job, motherfuckers.*

Keeping cool on the surface, I mind my gait on the way off the mound. Like it's easy. No sweat. It's all part of the mind game. But I'm on fire on the inside, burning up with a satisfied adrenaline as I walk off the field to the cheers and chants of everyone—except that same brunette who still has her nose in a book.

I'm unsettled suddenly that it's bothering me. Why do I care that her attention isn't on me? Stepping onto the dugout's top step, I lean against the rail, looking over the roof of the dugout to where the crowd has retaken their seats, heads swiveled to home where Gunner steps up to the plate. My only consolation is she still hasn't looked up. So it's not just one of my most important pitching days of my entire career that she's uninterested in. All I can say is it must be a damn good book.

3

AVERY

"Now would be a good time to take a peek at the game," Bodie informs me.

"Nah. I'm good."

I flip the page of my paperback as Bodie leans in closer. "Really, you should take a peek because Carter Barlowe keeps looking this way."

Lowering the book, I glance straight ahead to find a pair of deep-brown eyes staring back over the dugout's roof. It takes a second for me to break the contact, looking back at my book. "He probably has family sitting around us. Your dad really did get you some good seats."

"Yep. They're Dad's friend's seats, but they're out of town this weekend."

"Lucky us," I mumble returning my focus to the romance that is much more interesting than the sporting event in front of me. "What quarter is it?"

"'Quarter,' seriously?" Bodie asks in frustration. "I really hope you're messing with me."

Unable to hide my smirk, I glance over at him. "Just let me know when it's halftime." I focus back on my book as he drapes his arm over my shoulder, pulling me in for a friendly kiss on the cheek.

"I'm gonna grab us something to drink." Bodie takes off, and I get lost in the pages. Only a few chants and shouts pull me out of the story here and there. One of the good things about growing up with three siblings and now teaching a swarm of teenagers is I've learned to block out distractions and concentrate on the task at hand.

Bodie returns with sodas and snacks in hand, bending down to hand me fries and a Dr. Pepper. He remains standing, I notice, joining in with the crowd whooping and hollering. It's either been two minutes or two innings when he finally plops back in his chair, I don't care because this book has gotten *hot*, and I've lost all track of time.

"Damn, Barlowe is on fire."

"That's good. Have you had enough of the *atmosphere* yet so we can head out?"

When he doesn't respond, I look over at him, knowing what's coming next. I've been duped into a full game. "There's bound to be some postgame interviews right here." He points at the field as I shake my head in defeat.

"I should've brought another book." Or grabbed my Kindle because it doesn't look like we're leaving anytime soon.

"I'll buy you more books as soon as the game is over."

"Deal." Might as well get some new books out of the guilt trip.

The "big game" continues around me, and I'm only vaguely aware of Bodie and his new friend—our enthusiastic neighbor—doing a macho chest bump as they shout about another hitless inning or strikeouts or some nonsense before sitting back down.

"Um, Avery. You really should look now."

"I'm good."

I feel a few taps on my shoulder from around me as Bodie leans over. "Look on the jumbotron."

"The what?" I ask, my eyes immediately finding my dumbfounded face on the oversized screen across the stadium. "What the hell?"

Bodie doesn't share my terror at the sight of my ginormous face as he joins in the howls around us.

"Barlowe's number one fan," the announcer booms over the stadium's speakers. None too soon, the fans to the left and right of us jump around, waving and blocking the intrusive camera's view of me on the screen.

Thankfully, the commotion dies down, and everyone focuses back on the game. "Why would they do that?"

"Probably because you're the only person here not paying attention to the game."

"Big freakin' deal." And apparently it is. As I glance to the field, I'm met with the same steely brown eyes on me. He's throwing a damn ball around. "The book is still better than anything happening on the field. But can you let me know if they show me again? Please."

"Oh, you'll know. Ready for your fifteen minutes of fame?"

"No. I want to be left alone for fifteen minutes so I can find out how this damn story ends." Lifting the book, I keep it in front of me but at an angle where I can see the screen. And fortunately, my face doesn't appear on it again even though I can feel the heat in my cheeks as I do my best to avoid the game and all the chaos surrounding me.

The torture is finally over after nine innings, but I could swear it was more like nineteen. Bodie has joined the small crowd waiting at the edge of the field near where a sports reporter is waiting to interview the star pitcher. I sigh deeply, aware that I'm now stuck waiting on Bodie to stop fangirling.

The book had a good ending, but now I'm bored out of my mind. Propping my feet on the dugout in front of me, I rest my cheek in my hand and close my eyes. The day's agenda is only half over because now we have to go shopping. I was already exhausted from staying up most the night, but as I doze off, I can't decide if the baseball game or the shopping trip will be the most dreadful part of the day. But as I recall my face on the screen, I decide quickly that the game is indeed the worst part.

4

CARTER

"Carter Barlowe." The reporter beams as she motions for me to step in front of the camera. It's the last place I like being, but it comes with the territory. "Seven innings on your first game back. No scoring runs after you stepped off the mound, either. Bringing the Coyotes a win on the second game of the regular season. How'd it feel to be back?"

"It felt great." And it did. Truly. I elaborate a little, thanking my teammates and coaches and expressing my happiness at being back in the starting rotation. I may be stalling a bit in order to brace for the question I know is coming, and the reporter doesn't disappoint.

"Your father pitched for the Coyotes for twelve record seasons. Were there any nerves coming in to live up to his legacy?"

Keeping a straight face, I say the generic answer I've always given when anyone says anything about my dad. "My dad definitely left his mark on the sport." *Among other things since he's a piece of shit off the field.* "But I just wanted to come out here and do my best for my teammates and the Coyote fans."

She asks a few more questions about growing up in Canaan Falls, and I'm able to easily avoid mentioning my dad in the response. Soon she wraps up, thanks me for my time, and moves on to interview another player who hit a two-run homer—the only run-scoring at bat of the game.

I notice the small gathering of fans, including a few kids waving their arms around to get my attention. Walking over, I sign a few baseballs, gloves, and a jersey, but my attention remains on the two guys standing on the periphery as they chat amongst themselves.

Glancing over my shoulder, I see the hazel-eyed temptress still in her seat, feet kicked up and her head propped on her hand, appearing sound asleep. *Temptress* is exactly the correct term for her. Even with her damn alluring eyes closed, she's pulling me in. One of the guys chatting was the one sitting next to her. And I patiently sign my way towards him.

"Great game, man." He offers his hand, and I return the handshake.

"Thanks. Your girlfriend doesn't seem quite as intrigued." And why is it that's still scratching on my nerves? I had one of the best starts of my career, and one person out of forty thousand not noticing is bothering the shit outta me.

"Oh yeah, Avery." He nods in her direction as he chuckles. "We're not dating. I roped her into coming. Best-friend bro code. She's not a fan. I mean … baseball fan, not that she's not a fan of yours. She isn't all that into sports in general."

Avery. "I noticed." A little more than I should've. A few of those points make me feel better, the most significant being that she's not his girlfriend. Which shouldn't matter in the least to me.

"I should probably wake her up," he laughs as I sign something else that's thrust in front of me.

"Allow me." I give the small crowd a smile. "I'll be right back."

Hopping over the waist-high wall, I maneuver over to the seats where she's as comfortably reclined as you can be in a hard, plastic stadium seat. Tilting my head, I watch as she stirs a bit before I plop in the seat next to her, my focus trailing up her tanned thighs. She sits up, rubbing her eyes while mine roam the soft-looking skin of her neck down to her chest where a delicate gold chain disappears, my fingers itching to trail along the same path. Shit. Since when are jean shorts and a button-down shirt so damn sexy? And more importantly, why is the clothing more appealing than any of the Coyote attire that every other fan was donning?

"It's about time," she says in a groggy voice.

"Great game, huh?" I grin as she turns a shocked expression to me. No way she'd expected to hear any voice other than that of her friend. At least I hold her attention for a few seconds before she gives me a once-over and jumps out of her chair.

"Yes. It was," she says, pulling her bag onto her shoulder and surveying the area, spotting her friend. She gives him a look, eyes going big like she's saying, *Why are you over there and I'm over here? Help me!*

He doesn't though, which thoroughly amuses me. Instead, he gives her a wave as he stands talking, all casual as you please. When she moves to walk away, I ask, "How would you know since you kept your nose in a book the entire time?"

She immediately halts, her shoulders stiff as she turns to glare at me. Out of all the things I expected to see on her face, annoyance wasn't one of them, and I can't help but smile as she says, "It was a really good book."

"Apparently not good enough to keep you awake." Why do I want to know what (or more like who) keeps her awake at night? Annnnnd why the hell am I effortlessly picturing one of the many ways *I'd* keep her up all night? Preferably under me, in a darkened bedroom, her eyes on mine, and her attention definitely not on a damn book.

"That's because I finished it."

"Glad you got your happy ending." As soon as it spills out of my mouth, a film reel flips through my mind of all the different ways she could finish, but from the look of hatred she's giving me, I doubt we're picturing the same happy ending.

"Ditto. Great game. Welcome to Canaan Falls and all that shit." She waves her hand around, dismissing me before turning to make her getaway.

"This is my hometown. I grew up here. How about you, Avery?" I want to know something about her, anything other than she loathes the very thing my life revolves around.

She gives me a wary look before glancing back to her friend, but he's still paying her no mind. "Yes. I grew up in Canaan Falls." She starts walking, calling over her shoulder. "I really have to go."

With that, she hurries over to her buddy, pulling at his arm. I have no idea what she's saying, but it's clear to anyone with eyes that she's bitching him out. And it's also clear I'm part of the problem when the dude's eyes dart to me. He's a good sport though and obviously used to being on the receiving end of her irritation since he gives me a happy wave to which she responds by pulling down his arm and lightly slapping his chest. The guy chuckles before she pivots and heads up the stairs leading out of the stadium.

Damn. Avery might not want anything to do with me or the sport I love, but she's definitely piqued my interest. And that hasn't happened with anyone or anything other than baseball, ever.

5

AVERY

"Peace offering." Bodie holds up the paper coffee cup as he bows his head down.

"Not forgiven," I say while carefully taking the paper cup from his hands, "but there's no point in letting a good cup of coffee go to waste."

His smile tells me he knows he's already exonerated, but that won't stop me from giving him a hard time, which was exactly what I'd done during our shopping trip yesterday.

"Come on. You know it wasn't all that bad. We got to meet Carter Barlowe. What more can you ask for?"

"A best friend who doesn't drag me to baseball games." Yes, meeting the baseball star had been … interesting. But being woken up by him while sleeping at the stadium wasn't exactly ideal. Especially since I ran off because his stupidly enticing eyes left me a blabbering mess.

"Eh, could be worse." He lifts his identical paper cup, drinking down a swallow. "Ready to go?"

"Yep." I grab my phone and follow him out the door. We head to my parents' house for our standing Sunday lunch.

Bodie's attendance is expected as much as mine or my siblings', but he hasn't made it too often lately.

Once we arrive at my parents', we make our way into the house. Upon pushing the door open, the smell of Mom's home cooking fills the air, making my mouth water.

"Anyone home?" Bodie calls out.

My younger sister, Presley, greets Bodie before she even looks at me. It's been more than obvious that she's had a thing for Bodie for, like, ever. But we learned the hard way that we didn't want the drama of dating a best friend's sibling after my relationship with Bodie's older brother crashed and burned in high school, resulting in Bodie and I fighting with each other more than anything.

Ignoring my sister, I breeze into the kitchen, moving into Mom's warm embrace as she tells me Dad will be home from the store in a few minutes. The feed store is closed on Sundays, but it never stops Dad from going in to wrap up things he wanted to get done during the week. If anyone asked me, I personally think it's always been his solace. With four kids running around for two decades and now a rambunctious grandkid added to the mix, I didn't blame him one bit. Though Mom thrives in the chaos, I get why Dad needs a little while to himself just to clear his mind and recharge for the week. Because as much as I've adapted to dealing with general bedlam, I truly recharge when it's finally silent and serene. I'm unnecessarily reminded that neither of those things will be happening at this house anytime soon when my nephew runs through the kitchen, yelling and charging straight for me.

"What're we running from?" I ask, scooping him up in my arms to wrap him in a secure hug.

"Him!" Finn shouts as I spot my brother rushing in our direction, a Nerf gun aimed our way.

"Seriously, Rhett?" I ask, turning Finn out of the line of

fire. "Do you really have nothing better to do other than torment children?"

"Nope." It doesn't surprise me in the least as the youngest child of four smiles, firing the Nerf bullet that strikes me in the back. "Besides, he started it. I was minding my own business, taking me a good nap when this happened." Rhett holds up his arm to show me where *buttface* is sloppily written in what appears to be permanent marker. And I know the guilty party as I hear Finn giggling at the sight of his artwork.

"Did you do that?" I ask, trying to bite back a smile.

Finn's grin answers as he looks up to me with his pleading puppy dog eyes. "Don't tell Mom."

"'Don't tell Mom' what?" Tessa asks as she enters the kitchen, looking to her son in my arms.

"Nothing," I say in unison with Rhett as he hides his arm from our oldest sister. Serious and no-nonsense, Tessa wouldn't be pleased to find out her son dished out some well-deserved payback to his uncle.

"Yes. Very convincing." Tessa joins Mom as she finishes fussing at Bodie for missing so many recent family gatherings.

Still holding the Nerf gun at his side, Rhett angles it upward with his wrist, firing a shot that strikes Bodie in the chest.

"What was that for?" Bodie rubs over the spot.

"For taking her to the game and not me. Really, bruh. Why?"

"She's prettier than you," Bodie retorts, shielding himself as Rhett takes aim and fires at him again. "And she doesn't shoot at me."

"Yeah, but I would've stayed awake during the game," Rhett laughs.

Swinging my hand, I lightly slap Bodie on the chest. "You told him?" It had been embarrassing enough when it was just between me and my best friend, now I'll have Rhett relentlessly teasing me about it for all eternity.

"No, I didn't." Bodie rubs his chest. "But y'all have your aim coordinated."

"Really, Avery. Carter Barlowe's return to the big league, and you read and nap the entire time?"

"Whatever." I shake my head as Finn wiggles in my arms. Leaning over, I whisper in his ear, "He really deserved it," before placing a smooch on his cheek and setting him down so he can take off running.

"This isn't over!" Rhett shouts after Finn as I watch the little rascal disappear around a corner. On my right, from my peripheral vision, I register Bodie waving his hands and when my eyes cut to him, he halts, trying to play it off like the chump that he is.

"She doesn't know," Rhett hoots, bending over as he holds his stomach. "This is great."

"What's going on?" I ask Bodie, but he simply shrugs with the most unconvincing "innocent" expression I've ever seen. Eyes wide, eyebrows nearly at his hairline, mouth hanging slightly open. Idiot. I look back to my jokester brother and know whatever it is, I won't share in on my little brother's delight.

"Don't worry, Avery, Bodie didn't tell me. He didn't have to." Rhett gives Bodie a grin before turning back to me, not wanting to miss the opportunity to reveal whatever the hell is going on. "ESPN did."

"What?" I shout louder than intended as everyone in the kitchen focuses on me. Whipping around, I turn to face Bodie. "What *the hell* is he talking about?"

"Don't worry, sis. The picture of you reading wasn't all that bad." Rhett saunters over to drape his arm around my shoulder. "But that one of you drooling in your sleep while Carter Barlowe stood over you—classic." Rhett holds up his phone, lo and behold, it's a picture of me sleeping while the Coyotes pitcher hovers in front of me with his head cocked to the side, staring down at me. *Shit.*

Shoving the phone back at my brother, I round on little Mr. Innocent, who apparently knew but didn't think it vital to inform me of this latest development. "Why didn't you tell me?"

"I was gonna ... later."

"Yeah. Much later."

"Oh, calm down." Presley waves me off as she folds her arms over her chest and glares at me. "It's not even a big deal."

"No, not to you because it's not your face plastered all over a nationally televised program."

"You can barely see your face in most of the other pictures ... because the book is ... blocking it." Bodie's explanation loses steam as I turn my death stare on him. "Not that that seems to be helpful to you. Really, it was a quick highlight in the game. They were just joking about you being Barlowe's biggest fan. I'm sure it'll all blow over soon. Probably already has. No one cares about this stuff."

"Yeah. Only all of the local news stations and most of the major sports outlets," Rhett adds.

"Damn it, dude. Shut up." Bodie throws a hand up in the air, waving Rhett off. Not that he's made much progress in calming me down, but he's smart enough to know Rhett is an ass and will continue to rile me up.

"Yesterday was supposed to be a simple shopping trip with my best friend, and now I'm the joke of the week because I dared to read a damn book at a baseball game."

"See, if Bodie had taken me instead, neither of you would be in this situation." Rhett winks at Bodie who just shakes his head.

"*Buttface* should've been written across your forehead to

21

give anyone who looks at you twice a fair warning." My insult falls upon deaf ears since my buffoon of a brother is enjoying my humiliation way too much.

"I'm really sorry, Avery." Bodie gives me a look that reminds me of Finn's puppy dog eyes. He knows I'll crack eventually, but it'll be afterwards when my face is no longer a sports highlight, and he's trying his best to make me feel better.

"Hey, y'all," Dad calls out, making his way around the room to greet everyone until he stops in front of me. "Read any good books lately?"

Rhett cackles. Bodie tucks his chin to his chest. Presley rolls her eyes. And I accept my dad's warm hug with a long exhale. All this over a stupid baseball game.

6

CARTER

Staring at the phone screen, I read the text again before clicking the power button and tossing the phone in my locker. I don't have to read the message because the words have been on repeat every moment since I received the message from my father yesterday. The two simple words were waiting on my phone when I stepped off the field yesterday. *Great game.* That's it. But that's all it took for him to get into my head. I knew he'd watch the game. But I didn't think he'd acknowledge it, or me.

Spinning the leather chair around from my locker, I lean back and look around the clubhouse. Why are my nerves worse today than when I pitched yesterday? Today's workout was great. My arm is good. My mind, not so much. And I don't know why. I've had plenty of experience putting him out of my head. He won't screw with me now.

"Hey, Lowe," Gunner says as he approaches his locker. "Think I can borrow your fan club president today since you're not gonna need the support?"

The question rubs me the wrong way. I don't mind the shit everyone keeps giving me. That I can handle, but I don't like him insinuating Avery would be up for grabs. "Nobody wants to see more oversized posters of your mug in the crowd."

"Speak for yourself." Gunner tilts his head to the side, pretending to check himself out in a nonexistent mirror in his locker. "You can't have too much of this perfection."

Brooks steps between us, thankfully adding some levity. "He probably jerks off at night to one of them."

I can't help but chuckle and agree with Brooks's assessment of the shortstop who has no problem boosting his own ego.

"You probably do it too. Don't ya?" Gunner winks at Brooks as he shakes his head. There's no point trying to jab at the guy who makes an ass of himself voluntarily, just for kicks. He can be a tool, but he definitely keeps the clubhouse on the livelier side.

"But for real, I require an audience with Ms. Barlowe Fan Club." Gunner points my way, giving me a look that hits me in my gut. I don't want him anywhere near Avery. Shit. *I* want an audience with her but seeing as I don't know anything other than her first name and the fact that she hates baseball—and seemingly, baseball players—there's jack shit to be done.

"You good?" Brooks asks without a look my way as he buttons his jersey.

"Yeah. Just ready to get out there again." Because I feel like it wasn't real, or maybe a lucky break. Surely it wasn't a one-time fluke. There's no way I'm only going to have one *great game* all season, right? Damn Cash Barlowe and his poisonous existence.

"You can have my spot," Brooks mumbles jokingly, but I get the feeling that he'd willingly give it up to me today if he could, or least I think it's only for today.

"Are *you* good?" I ask.

He stops situating his uniform for a few seconds before resuming. "Yeah. Just an off day."

"We all have them."

"Yep." Brooks remains silent as I make a mental note to keep an eye on him. I don't know much about the rookie third baseman, but I know he seems to be having a lot more off days than normal, especially considering how well he'd performed in spring training.

I call his name as he walks away, then he turns to look over his shoulder at me. "You've got my number. Feel free to use it if you need to." He nods, tension in his posture, but I also clock the grateful expression on his face.

Grabbing my phone, I erase the text from my dad. Outta sight, outta mind? Here's hoping. Then, I pull up the article with the picture of me staring at Avery—I don't care to admit how much I've focused on that snapshot. In reality, I'd only stood there a few seconds, but the photographer captured the moment between us forever; it's now frozen in my mind for eternity. The fact that I'm the ass of the joke should make me loathe the picture, but all I see is her. Damn it. All I've seen since she ran off were those damn hazel eyes.

Closing out the picture, I dial my agent. Joe's always been more of a friend than "my agent," but he still has to do damage control when things go the wrong way (i.e., not the way *he* wants them to go). He says my image sells more than my playing, and we've never seen eye to eye on that. I detest that my father is attached to my image whether I like it or not.

"It's about time," Joe bitches.

"Been a little busy." *A little busy avoiding your phone calls and texts because I knew you'd bawl me out.*

"You're lucky you pay me a lot."

"Yeah, that's lucky for you too. What's up?"

"Lowe. You know what's up. How could you not give me

a heads-up or something so I could get in front of the story instead of them blasting photos of the two of you?"

"There was nothing to get in front of."

"So, you don't know her?"

"Nope." And that really bugs me more than any of this shit. "Just met her yesterday."

"Okay. Well, the good news is it's not hurting your image, rather giving you a more human element."

"Great." I hate that word now. *Thanks, Dad.*

"Yeah. I'd usually say let's send her a jersey or a fruit basket or something, but I doubt she'd care." He can't even get through the sentence without snickering.

"You too, huh?" Is there anyone who doesn't plan on taking a few jabs about her not giving a shit about me or my return?

"Yeah. It *is* nice that one person in the world isn't obsessed with Carter Barlowe. At least, as long as she doesn't get others to follow along."

"Well, I'm sure you two would get along *great*." Send her something, huh? "Any clue on where we'd deliver our thanks-for-making-an-ass-out-of-Barlowe memorabilia?"

"Canaan Falls West High School. Ms. Avery Whitlock, history teacher."

That doesn't surprise me but rather fits her somehow. "You really did your research."

"It's my job to know everything and anything that affects you, and Avery Whitlock joined that list yesterday. But it wasn't that hard to find out. There were a few comments on a social media post about her being their teacher. But that answers my other question of whether you knew if she'd attend more games."

"I doubt it."

"Good deal. Call me after the game. We need to schedule

a few things." Joe pauses before he says, "There's a request for an interview with your father."

"Never gonna happen."

"That's what I thought, but I had to double check before I told them no again." Joe knows the drill because he's one of the few people who knows the real Cash Barlowe. "Talk to you later. Seriously, call me tonight. We still have some stuff to go over."

"Got it." I disconnect the call and sit in a daze until it's time to head to the dugout. The stadium isn't as full as it was yesterday, but there's still a good-sized crowd in attendance. So, why do my eyes search the same spot Avery sat yesterday? I hope to find hazel eyes staring back at me, but of course she isn't there.

The few moments my dad hasn't been in the forefront of my mind are the moments I've focused on her, and that's what I plan to continue doing. Not that I have a choice, though. Because having a choice implies control, the making of a decision, and having a plan indicates thoughtful execution of achieving a specific result. Neither of those things describe the compulsive way my eyes automatically seek her out in the crowd, only to come up empty each time. Spotting only unfamiliar faces, I'm man enough to admit I crave the one that wants nothing to do with me. But maybe I can change that.

7

AVERY

"Good morning."

My greeting is returned by most students as they arrive to class. Others give me a quick nod and slip into their seats. That's fine; Mondays are hard for some, so I don't take any of it personal. Plus, first period is usually the quietest, except for one student who is at full volume despite the early hour.

My phone vibrates on my desktop, and I know it's from Bodie before I even look. He's been apologizing nonstop. And even though I know he's not directly responsible, I still want to forget all about it.

Bodie: Supper's on me tonight. Your pick. What are we having?

Me: Doesn't matter to me.

Bodie: Are you sure? I figured you'd choose something expensive as a means to make me pay restitution.

Me: I should, but you can just pick up something.

As I note the time, I drop my phone into the drawer and look around the classroom. A few sets of eyes watch me, and I've had my fingers crossed all morning that there's not too many baseball fans among my students. That wishful thinking is instantly demolished as E.J. walks in and shouts, "Ms. W, how you gonna do my boy like that?"

"Have a seat, E.J."

He grins, walking over to my desk. Flashing the picture of me sleeping at the game, he says, "Now you know how I feel about history."

"Sit. Now." My lips form a tight line as I stare at him. He's right on par with being first period's most entertaining student, but this isn't something I want to entertain.

"Yes, ma'am. But can you at least get his autograph or something for me?"

"No, I can't. I don't know him, despite what that looks like." I point to the device in his hand. "Put the phone away before it stays with me for the day."

"Do you have his phone number?"

When I give him my that's-enough-E.J. look, he holds his hands up and laughs, heading to his seat. "Just thought I'd try. Anyone else would've taken advantage of meeting Carter Barlowe."

Yes. I'm sure they would've, and I've heard the same sentiment ad nauseam—especially from Rhett. He'd kept questioning me and Bodie throughout lunch yesterday even though I kept insisting there was nothing to tell. Grabbing my cell, I quickly type a message.

Me: My student wants an autograph and Carter's phone number.

Bodie: You should've asked for them.

Me: Shut up. And on second thought, you'd better bring a big-ass bottle of wine and an extravagant meal tonight.

Tucking my cell away, I focus on starting the day's lesson. It might all be in my mind, but the longer class goes on, the more everyone in it seems distracted. Or maybe it's just me. Attempting to get back on track is pointless, especially when there's a knock on the door.

I'm utterly dumbstruck when Principal Newman walks in with none other than Carter Barlowe. *What in the actual hell is going on?*

"Good morning, Ms. Whitlock," Principal Newman beams.

Why is Carter here? Is he mad about being a laughingstock? Is he here to get me fired? How did he even find me? I'm physically unable to respond. Like a complete halfwit.

There're several gasps and whispers around the classroom before I hear E.J.'s way too loud, "Yo, I thought you didn't know him, Ms. W?"

"I don't," I finally say as steadily as possible. Managing the world's fakest smile, I focus on my boss and ignore Mr. Bruised Ego beside him. "Good morning, sir. Is everything all right?" I make the mistake of looking directly into the sun. The smile Carter Barlowe flashes me is so bright it's nearly blinding. He's got to be here for a reason—whether that reason is me or this is purely coincidental, I've not a clue—but he's incontrovertibly delighted with my obvious alarm at his surprise visit.

"Oh, yes. Everything is fantastic. Mr. Barlowe wanted a tour of the school and asked specifically for a visit to your classroom."

"How nice of him." I literally clench my teeth, pressing my tongue up against the backs of them to keep from adding a few extra words. The sarcastic comment hidden within my polite response isn't lost on Carter as his smile grows. And even if it's attached to his gorgeously symmetrical face, I still want to deck him in his perfect nose. He doesn't need his face intact in order to work, he only throws a damn baseball around for a living.

"Can I get an autograph now?" E.J. asks, beginning to stand up of his desk.

"Stay in your seat, Ernest."

All I need is to lose control of the class and have them swarm Principal Newman in an effort to get to Carter. Although, that might be a good plan to get him out of my classroom.

"How you gonna do me like that in front of my boy?" E.J. asks, shaking his head as he plops back on to his seat. Our agreement is I call him by his preferred nickname if he behaves in my class. And since he's the ringleader, I really need him to listen.

Carter, on the other hand, looks like he's not bothered by the disruption one bit. "I don't mind signing some autographs while I'm here."

"Can I get your phone number?" E.J. asks. I close my eyes, my fingers pressing against my temple momentarily before I look at my student. "What? I figured I'd shoot my shot. It's Carter freakin' Barlowe."

Yes. I don't need to be reminded. Again.

Carter walks over to E.J., cool and casual, as all eyes watch him. E.J. pulls out a Coyotes jersey that has *Barlowe* stamped on the back of it. He'd really been prepared.

"I'm E.J., not Ernest," E.J. gives me an annoyed look before focusing back to Carter. "Man, you're my favorite player ever. You're the best the Coyotes—the league!—has ever had." E.J. continues his starstruck rambling while Carter signs the jersey then leans in to pose for a selfie with E.J. before giving him a pat on the shoulder.

Carter pivots to the chair beside E.J. where a student holds out a notebook with a pleading look. As Carter signs it, Jackie says, "You and your dad are so awesome."

"Cash Barlowe is a punk-ass bitch," E.J. retorts with zero hesitation.

"*Ernest—*" I'm ready to lay into E.J. (in a professional and appropriate manner) but Carter holds up his hand, halting me.

31

There's a slight smile peeking at Carter's mouth. "Everyone is entitled to their own opinion."

"Yep," E.J. agrees.

I stand near E.J., wondering what will come out of his mouth next and pondering how Carter does this day in and out with a smile on his face. Though he moves efficiently (and charmingly, damn it) around my classroom, signing something for every single student, it doesn't stop me from wanting to strangle him for showing up in the first place and "specifically" asking to visit my classroom.

When he's made it to the last student, Principal Newman says, "We can continue the tour," and gestures with an open hand to the door.

"I was hoping Ms. Whitlock could show me around," Carter informs Mr. Newman.

Do not roll your eyes, Avery. Do not roll your eyes. I know for a fact not a thing changes on my face. There's no way in hell I'll give him the satisfaction. Unfortunately, I'm so focused on maintaining my expression that I feel my right hand form a tight fist unbidden. It happens for only a moment before I register the tension and relax it. But Carter's perceptive eyes dart down—the man is used to reading the slightest of hand signals for a living, for crying out loud—and when his eyes meet mine again, I see recognition in them. *Busted.* Ugh.

"I can get someone to watch her classroom, not a problem," Principal Newman appeases.

Him going out of his way to accommodate the star player rubs me completely the wrong way. No one else would be allowed to stroll onto campus and disrupt a teacher's schedule.

"That's not necessary. I'm sure Mr. Barlowe will benefit exponentially from touring with you, or perhaps he can engage in a self-guided tour."

"Nonsense. It's no trouble at all. When is your free period?" my principal asks me, and I know Carter has success-fully enlisted me as his stupid tour guide of Canaan Falls West High School whether I want to participate or not.

"Next period, sir," I grit out.

Principal Newman glances at his watch. "Perfect. There's about ten minutes until the bell. I can watch the room until then."

"Oh, no. That's okay." Our school's leader has completely lost his mind, so I look to Carter. "I'll just catch up in a few." *Go on, git,* as my granddaddy used to say. *Don't let the door hit ya where the good Lord split ya.*

"I'll just hang out here and watch you in action." And then this jerk winks at me.

I only thought I wanted to deck him in the nose before. Now, it's tenfold as he strolls to the back of the room and takes a seat at an empty desk that is too small for his large frame—beside E.J. of all students.

"Wonderful," I mutter under my breath, knowing the next ten minutes are going to feel longer than the nine innings of baseball I sat through.

"Be sure and stop by my office before you head out." Principal Newman exits the room, leaving me with a class where all eyes are pointed at Carter in the rear of the room.

"Okay. Where were we?" Because I have no freakin' clue. Looking around, I see most of the attention has stayed glued on Carter. There's no way I'll be able to teach with him in the room. "Since class is almost over, let's take some quiet time to get started on homework." And for me to get a grip.

Quickly, I grab my phone from the drawer of the desk I sit behind.

Me: Change of plans. Bring something stronger than wine.

Bodie: Um. Why? Did a student ask for your autograph or something?

Me: Carter Barlowe is HERE.

Bodie: What? Why?

Me: I don't know. He wants a tour of campus and Newman is apparently a big fan of his.

Bodie: Okay. Let me know how it goes. I'll be at the liquor store if you need anything else.

There's nothing there that can help me deal with Carter right now. Unless there's a time machine he could find me. I'd go back and say no to that stupid game in a heartbeat. As if he knows I'm thinking about him, I look up to meet an amused expression on Carter's face as he stares at me. Ballsy.

Yes. He's definitely won this round, and we both know it because there's no way I can run off and get away from him. And I'll be damned if part of me doesn't want to stick around to find out if there's something under that arrogant grin, anyway.

8

CARTER

This has turned out to be even better than I expected as I watch her across the room. The principal was too happy to sign me in as a guest and had no problem ushering me right to her classroom. The shock on her face was priceless. But now, it looks more like loathing. Feisty. I can work with that.

E.J. leans over and whispers, "You should shoot your shot too. She's really cool for a teacher."

"I'm not sure it would go well."

"Probably not." He snickers and glances over to Avery as she does her best to avoid looking in my direction. There's an obvious connection between her and the kid. He's definitely the class clown and probably a tad of a troublemaker, but she seems to be on his good side. That says a lot. And so does his assessment of my father. He won me over right away by seeing straight through the bullshit of the dog and pony show my father puts on.

"She's not like the other teachers. She's better." The kid speaks with a heartfelt sincerity that makes me want to get to know everything about her and learn firsthand how she earned his respect.

"So, you play ball?" I ask.

"I used to, but work has to come first now." E.J. shakes his head.

Work? He can't be more than fifteen or sixteen years old. And it's moments like this that I feel like a prick for not appreciating the luxuries that I was provided by my father even if they came with their own price. "Well, maybe if you have some time off, you can come to a game."

His face immediately lights up, and I'm already making a mental note to get him tickets. "Really? That'd be amazing. I promise to not read or sleep during the game." His reassurance is convincing and hilarious as he nods happily.

"Thanks, bud."

We chat baseball until the bell rings, then he instructs me not to screw up with Ms. W before walking over to her. The other students rise out of their seats, some waving, some plain old staring at me until they all eventually make their way out to the hallway, leaving me and Avery in the empty classroom.

"What are you doing here?" Her tone is flat, but I see the frustration in her posture as she rises from her desk and folds her arms over her chest.

"You visited me at work, figured I'd return the favor." I can't help but enjoy her growing frustration. I relish in it when she gives up her calm demeanor and throws her hands in the air.

"You're a baseball player. An audience is part of the job description for you. It's not in mine. How did you find out where I worked, anyway?"

"I have my ways." *Thank you, Joe.* This is far more enjoyable than showing up at the field hours early because it's better than staring at the bare walls of my new house in the town I never thought I'd return to again.

"Yes, I'm sure you do. You proved your point. So you can leave now."

"What point is that?" I ask curiously, wanting to know what she thinks I'm up to because I'm not even sure anymore.

"That you're in control and can make my life miserable all because I wasn't interested in your infantile game." She walks over to me, leaning over the desk as she glares to me. "So, if you plan to get me fired, go ahead and try."

Fired? "Why would I want to get you fired? I just wanted a tour from Ms. W, and apparently she's the best teacher around—according to E.J."

"You can't be happy with the pictures and everyone making the *both* of us out to be a joke."

"I'd say the joke's on them." Because I sure as hell don't mind since it's the reason Joe was able to find out who she is.

"Don't you have a game or practice or, like, weight lifting or some sort of *sporty* thing—you know, somewhere *else*— that you need to get to?"

"I have time." Plenty of time for her. I don't have to be at the field for a few hours, and even so, I have a feeling I'd make the time even if I didn't have it. Something doesn't sit right about that with me. What is it about her? I want to get to know her. What am I looking for, though? And what happens when I find it?

"I don't."

"Avery, just a few minutes. Show me around the school, tell me a little bit about how you won over the class clown who is usually labeled the problematic student, and I'll tell Principal Newman that you were the most gracious tour guide ever— even if you do hate me and try to shove me over the landing."

"It's a thought." Her expression softens a bit as she moves behind her desk, grabbing keys and her phone out of the drawer. Softly she says, "I don't hate you. I just don't understand why you're here."

I don't understand, either. But I hope to figure it—and her—out soon. Rising out of the cramped desk, I stretch and give her a smile. "Lead the way."

The brief glimpse I got of her at ease is gone as she shakes her head and walks out of the classroom, locking the door behind us. Mechanically, she walks through the hallway, pointing out various things as she names them. Once we make our way around to the gym, she points at the double doorway, and I peek through the window. Coeds are playing basketball during PE—some three-on-three is happening on one side of the court and another group is practicing free throws on the other side while some others linger in the bleachers. "Looks like fun."

"You said you grew up in Canaan Falls?"

"I did. But my dad made me go to a private school."

"You act like it's a bad thing."

"It wasn't. I just didn't want to do anything he wanted me to do, solely because he wanted me to do it."

"So, why do you play his sport then?"

For the first time in my life, I confess the truth out loud, admit where my original passion for the game ignited. "Because he didn't want me to."

She gives me a puzzled look. "But you're playing for his team."

"It was the organization that wanted to sign me. And at the end of the day, I just wanted to be on the mound again." I take in a deep breath as I glance around the gymnasium hallway. "It started out as a way to piss him off. But I found being on the field was the only place I wanted to be. For me, not him." My gaze meets hers to find curiosity brewing. "My father was a hell of a baseball player, but E.J. wasn't wrong in his assessment of the man I knew off the field. And I'd appreciate it if you kept that to yourself." Did I really admit that aloud to her? Shit, I'm unsure if I'm testing her or myself. Because I can count on one hand how many people know my true feelings about my father.

She gives me a knowing nod, her eyes locked on mine, and it's in that moment that I know I don't need to worry one bit that she'd betray my confidence or sell me out for some news story payout and a few minutes of fame.

Leading me down a corridor, she opens a door, and we enter the cafeteria. She points around, telling me that it used to be half the size before the addition was added on a few years ago.

"So, you attended high school here?" I fish for intel but only receive a nod as confirmation. She's not so willing to share, but I hope I can change that eventually. "What made you decide to become a history teacher?"

Her eyes land on me, narrowing for a split second before she looks ahead and leads me out of the lunchroom. "I always wanted to be a teacher. I loved school. And as cliché as it sounds, I wanted to make a difference for the students like E.J. who I don't see as problematic but who need some extra guidance in the right direction sometimes."

"He's a great kid."

"He is."

"He gave me a bit of advice." I take in a deep breath, internally laughing at myself for being nervous as I say, "He told me I should 'shoot my shot.'"

Avery's response is to pick up her pace, but as we round the corner, I recognize the school's entryway which is really close to the principal's office—where she is heading with purpose.

"I have a feeling he and I will both be disappointed if I don't heed his advice," I say as she halts, slowly turning to face me. "So, can I get your number or maybe meet you sometime for coffee?"

The horror on her face isn't exactly what I'd expected. The look does nothing but kick up a churning in my gut. It intensifies when she shakes her head and responds, "No. I don't think that's a good idea."

Shit. I did. I still do. "And what makes you think that?"

"History. That's what," she responds, ushering me into the main office, making her way to the secretary's desk. "Principal Newman wanted to see Mr. Barlowe before he left, but I really need to get back to my classroom. Can you show him to his office?"

The secretary hurriedly jumps up, as eager to help as Avery is to escape me. "Avery." When I say her name, she stops, quickly glancing over her shoulder with a mixture of uncertainty and something else I can't quite read on her face.

"It was really nice to meet you, Carter, but I have to get back to my students." With that, she walks away, and I stand there, watching her once again hurry away. Only this time, I feel like she's running from me in particular and not just some baseball player she assumed the worst about.

"Right this way, Mr. Barlowe." The giddy lady speaks with such sweetness that I have to return her smile, but I'm defeated inside. My shot didn't get anywhere near the desired goal. I told E.J. I didn't think it'd go well, but that was before I felt like there was a real connection between me and Avery. Or maybe that feeling was some kind of release from blubbering about my family issues. One thing is for sure though, the great Wayne Gretzky had it right: "You miss one hundred percent of the shots you don't take." And Avery Whitlock is worth taking a few more cracks at even if I know I'll strike out a few times. And I'm sure I will.

The tantalizing temptress has me so twisted up in her trance, I'm quoting hockey players and have given up control of the game to her. She's the one on the mound, determined to strike me out and send my ass back to the dugout. But she hasn't done her research, her stats on me are zip. Which means she doesn't know what she's up against. Which gives me a chance. I'm smart and damn well determined when my head is in the game. And right now, it's consumed with scoring an opportunity to discover more about the beauty hiding behind those hazel eyes. So, I've got a few more swings left. My time in the batter's box isn't up yet. *Make it count, Barlowe.*

9

AVERY

I pull the front door of my apartment open. "You're late."

Bodie holds up several bags. "That's because I went to every place that I could remember you liked within a thirty-mile radius."

"You didn't have to," I say, feeling guilty and exhausted after fussing at him on the phone earlier. "It was just a long day."

"Yeah. Of touring the school with a famous baseball player."

I glare at him as he sets the bags on the counter and holds his hands out in defeat. "Really though, Avery. Is it such a bad thing that Carter Barlowe wants to hang out with you?"

"Yes. Because anyone you refer to by their full name isn't someone who *hangs out* with people like me. I'm a challenge. That's all. The one who dared not be entertained by watching him play catch for three hours." That has to be why. It's the only thing I can think of that would make Carter pursue me. And I'm guessing my lack of interest and the media making a joke of it, memes included, isn't helping Mr. Big Shot's ego. Although, there were a few minutes where I saw something different in him. And as much as I wanted to cling to that, at the end of the day, we're worlds apart. "He's a professional athlete. And I'm just ... me."

"Avery, stop. Maybe he wants to get to know you because you're you."

Shaking my head, I reach into the to-go sack I recognize from my favorite Italian eatery. "Can we talk about something else, please?"

"So, you're not going to fuss at me in your teacher-Avery voice for everything?"

"No. I just want to forget." I plunk down on the sofa, digging my fork into the pasta dish that smells delightful.

"That can be arranged," Bodie holds up a bottle of liquor, then a beat later, he pulls out a bottle of wine. "But it's a school night, so I brought this too."

"Good thinking."

He moves around my small kitchen, grabbing two glasses, uncorking the bottle before pouring us both a healthy serving. Setting my glass on the coffee table, he sits on the sofa next to me. Grabbing the remote, he clicks the TV on, tuning into the Coyotes game, of all things. When I turn a glare on him, he says, "Your man isn't even pitching tonight, Avery."

"Okay. What part of 'forget' are you unclear on? Besides, he's not *my* man." He's nothing to me.

"This is about my brother," Bodie says. I stop and look to him, hating and loving that I don't have to explain myself to my best friend. "He's not the same. Besides, that was like seven years ago. High school, Avery. Carter is in a completely different league than Russell ever was. Literally." He gently pats my knee.

"I know. But it's more than that." It's a lot more than the fact that I swore off jocks after Russell cheated on me and used football practice as his main cover. "Carter is in a different league altogether. He attended private school, grew up in the same town as us but in a completely different life. He's famous. All I want to do is hide out in my apartment, eat pasta, and teach my students. Maybe enjoy a good book or two—in peace, not on the jumbotron at the stadium."

"I get it, Avery." Bodie leans over, draping his arm over my shoulder. "But I still think you're selling us short."

"*Us?*"

"Yeah. I bet he would totally do an interview for my podcast if y'all were dating."

Jabbing my fingers into his side, he recoils, laughing before hauling me closer.

"I'm joking, mostly, but I still think you're selling yourself short. *He'd* be the lucky one to snag you, not the other way around."

I give Bodie a heartfelt smooch on the cheek, then lean my head on his shoulder. "I'm still mad at you. This is all your fault, but I'm glad you finally have time to hang out."

"Me too." He kisses the top of my head as I watch the screen, and even though Mr. Comeback's not pitching, I watch for him anyway. Scanning the dugout for his stupid face any time the camera pans that way. And I'm rewarded a few times with quick glimpses of him alternately smiling and laughing with a teammate, leaning on the railing while squinting out at the field, and spitting directly onto the ground in a way that should be disgusting and crude yet strikes me as casual and commonplace … maybe a hair shy of sexy. Which may be the strangest thing I've ever thought. Ugh. Who in their right mind would find expectorating the least bit attractive?

What he said about his dad rings in my head. From what I know (and read after a brief round of Internet research), Cash Barlowe is a local and much-worshipped hero. I couldn't find anything that said any different. Even in Carter's interview clips that I watched (purely for informational purposes), he gives the same generic answers about his father being a great ball player.

How different was Mr. Big League off the field? Because the man that flashes on my TV screen appears cocky; an arrogant pitcher who has the world at his fingertips. But today, in the gym hallway at Canaan Falls West High School, he was just Carter—a normal guy who I typically would have given a chance, had a cup of coffee with, and seen where it went. But the guy on TV is part of him too, and I don't know which one is the real Carter.

10

CARTER

It's been all of forty-eight hours since I walked this same corridor with Avery, and here I am, anxiously making my way to her, unable to get there fast enough. Thanks to the principal on Monday, I'm already in the school system's visitor registry, so I only had to sign the log in the front office to receive my visitor tag. The principal offered to accompany me again, but I told him I'd stop by after I check in with Avery during her free period. Shit. Already having memorized part of her schedule is a clear indicator that I'm a goner.

Stopping in front of her classroom, I peek through the doorway and spot her sitting at her desk. She's gorgeous as she concentrates on the papers in front of her, busily writing away. She looks so peaceful. Serene and in her element. And I'm about to destroy that. But I'm determined to convince her to give me a chance, even if I have to tick her off a few times.

Stepping through the doorway, I do my best to maintain her calm vibe. When her eyes dart to me, I clock the shock first before the annoyance covers her face. She lifts a finger to her mouth, telling me to be quiet, before pointing to the back of her classroom. As I move stealthily towards her desk, I spot E.J. sound asleep in his chair.

"I see you put people to sleep at your job too," I whisper.

"What do you want?" she murmurs in a hushed tone while glowering at me.

"Coffee. With you." I gesture with the cardboard carrier I hold containing two paper cups and sack filled with pastries that I normally wouldn't indulge in. "Danishes and croissants. Warm and toasted."

"You really need to find a hobby or something because you obviously have too much free time on your hands," she hisses, looking away.

I reach her desk and set the hot beverages down. I'm counting this as a win for now because she hasn't actually told me to leave. Yet. But that might come soon judging by the frustration flashing across her face. She resumes her task, head down, marking across the paper on her desktop.

I pluck a cup from the carrier and slide it closer to her. "I didn't know what you take in your coffee so I brought a little of everything." I offer her the paper sack full of cream and sugar.

She hesitates, then accepts it from me. "Thank you." I'm close enough where she's not exactly whispering anymore but has instead adopted this quiet sort of raspy purr. And it's hot as hell. "Although I still don't understand what you're doing here."

Ditto. "It looks like he needs this more than me." I nod at the other cup in the carrier. I hadn't taken a drink from it since I'd been hurrying to get here, and now I'm grateful. "Are you really just letting him sleep through school?" I know it's been a while since I've been a student but sleeping through second period seems like a no-go regardless of graduation year.

She casts a sympathetic glance his way as she whispers, "He wasn't himself when he walked in today and looked exhausted, so I let him sleep. I'd do the same for any of my students. I don't know what they're dealing with at home, and sometimes there's more behind them being sleepy than I could ever imagine. I'd rather let them rest while they can for a few minutes than lecture them about a history lesson that will still be available when they wake up."

"Wow," I breathe. Instinctively, I raise my hand to brush my thumb across her cheek. "He was right. You really are the best teacher."

She tenses and I yank my hand away as she moves back slightly, taking a quick peek at E.J. before softly saying, "I just know there's more to school and life than memorizing time-lines and names. It's very out of character for him to not come in loud and keep everyone smiling." Her gaze travels back to him, hunched over, head resting on crossed arms on the desktop, the worry she feels for her student is palpable.

"Avery," I whisper as she turns to me, "do you think there's something bad going on at home?"

"I don't know. I do know he works outside of school. A few weeks ago, he was in a grouchy mood, so unlike his usually playful self, but when I broached the subject, he immediately shut the conversation down. Said he was just tired. I have to take him at his word and trust that he'll come to me if he needs to. And I hope he will, so I don't push … because I worry if I push too hard, he won't feel comfortable with me when he really does need someone."

"Do you need someone?" The question tumbles out before I can stop it, earning a baffled expression from her. Yeah, I can't believe I asked it either.

"I'm fine."

"I'm sure you are." I'm obviously not. Time for a subject change. "How do you take your coffee?"

"I'll fix it." I watch her put cream and sugar into the cup before stirring it. She doesn't resume grading papers but instead leans back in her chair and looks up at me. "You can't keep showing up here. I'm going to get in trouble even if you are the principal's pet."

The atmosphere relaxes a bit as I let out a breath. Spotting an extra chair a few paces away, I nod toward it. "Mind?" Her eyes follow, landing on the chair. Blinking slowly, she nods once. In a flash, I grab the chair and silently place it beside her desk before sitting. "I bet you speak from experience. Teacher's pet in school?"

She gives me a stare and eye squint that confirms I've hit the nail on the head. "And I bet you were the jock who never showed up for class but always managed to ace every test. Miraculously, you always maintained your eligibility to play ball."

Damn. She really does have a low opinion of athletes. And it's clear I'm not the original source of it. "Is that assessment from personal experience or just a blanket assumption of meatheads in general?"

"More personal experience than I care to admit, but thankfully ancient history."

"Can't be too *ancient* if it's still riling you up now. But I wouldn't label myself a jock anyways. I did show up for all my classes because I planned to attend university. My dad's alma mater's bitter rival. So, no meathead pass for me because I was determined to get accepted."

"You really went out of your way to make him angry."

"Yep."

"Did it work?"

"Yep. And I graduated with a degree in business, so I had a backup plan in case ball didn't pan out."

"Looks like you didn't need that backup after all."

I unconsciously rub my right elbow. "Never know. My

career could end tonight, or next week, or five years from now. Nothing is certain." She breaks eye contact, glancing across the room, but my gut says she just wanted to look away from me. "How about you? I'm guessing you didn't rebel much."

She smiles, nodding her head. "I didn't have to. That role was filled by my little brother."

"Brother? I'm an only child. I always wanted a brother."

"Well, I have one brother and two sisters. I love them but wanted some peace and quiet growing up—and my own bathroom."

"A quiet, empty house is overrated." In childhood and adulthood. Although, the latter hasn't ever bothered me much until recently.

"What about your mom? Does she still live in Canaan Falls?"

Her asking me a question is a good thing, shows at least a tad of interest on her part. Maybe I'm successfully prying my way into her hard shell after all. But out of all the topics, family isn't the one I'd pick for first-coffee-date topics. Is this a date? Damn, I hope so. "Yes, she's still here, but we don't have much contact."

"Why not?"

Normally, I'd hesitate to answer, instead I respond easily to Avery. "Because she never put a stop to my dad's behavior, so I resented her equally for his actions. Even though she was on the receiving end too."

"Oh, I shouldn't have pried," Avery says, pink staining her cheeks.

"It's okay. I blamed her, but I still defended her as soon as I was able to. And as soon as I could, I got her away from him permanently. I blamed her, but I wanted her safe. Now she is."

"I'm sorry." Avery glances down to the cup in her hand as she takes a sip.

"Never apologize to me," I utter. I hate that everyone has always been so quick to placate and accommodate me. I just want them to call me on my shit, like the feisty part of Avery I've seen. "Unless it's for sleeping through my game."

Her posture relaxes and she rolls her eyes. "I tried, but those damn nineteen innings lasted *forever*."

"At least you were able to finish your book."

"Mm-hmm." She smiles as a muffled snore comes from E.J.'s direction.

"Why were you at the game if you hate baseball so much?"

"Bodie guilted me into going. The plan was to spend some quality time together. And it was only supposed to be for a few innings which turned into the entire game and then all the fangirling afterwards. That's when I kinda dozed off."

"'Quality time'? Reading and sleeping?" I'm teasing, but there's one thing that I'm dead serious about. "Well, I owe Bodie one hell of a thank you for bringing you along."

We're both smiling, each of us in on the falling-asleep joke, but I watch the smile fall from her lips and hear her breath catch as her eyes dart down to my mouth. Intuitively, I lean in, and those strikingly mesmerizing dark-hazel eyes snap to mine. This is it. The moment where the ball is headed out of the park, over the left-field wall as she slightly leans towards me. When a gargled snore catches her attention, she quickly shifts away from me. Damn it. Strike.

"You should go," she whispers, sliding her coffee away from her and picking up her pen.

"What time is it?" E.J. blurts, startling awake. Glancing around the empty classroom, he focuses on us sitting at the front of the room. "Oh, shit. I can't be marked absent. I've missed too much school already." The poor kid starts jamming his stuff into a backpack as Avery stands.

"It's all right. I sent a note to Mrs. Smith letting her know that you were staying in my classroom."

"She's not gonna tell the office I skipped class, right?"

"No, you're good, E.J. You can hang in here or head to her room if you want. There's not much time left, though."

Not much time left. That hits me funny. Why do I feel that deep down?

"I'll hang here then." E.J. focuses in on me, rubbing the sleep from his eyes as he yawns. "Ms. W, you sure do visit a lot with someone you don't know. Or did he shoot his shot and score?"

Oh, I dig this kid, even if he's wrong.

"We're *not* having this conversation," Avery instructs him as he snickers.

"I meant to give this to you," I reach into my wallet, pulling out one of the ridiculous business cards Joe had printed for me. And it's the first one I've given out. Flipping it over, I gesture for Avery's pen, jot down my cell number on the back, then walk over and hand it to E.J. "If you ever need anything, give me a call."

"Are you legit?" E.J. asks, his eyes wide as he studies the card like it's a magical key to a parallel universe.

"Yep. And I'd better not find this on the Internet, *Ernest.*"

"No chance. Unless you keep calling me that stupid name."

I laugh and bite back the unusual urge to ruffle his hair. It would be weird to do—the kid's way too old and I barely know him. But then again, he is still a kid. And I have a deep sense that he truly needs that kind of affection in his life. Weird. I dunno where the hell this is coming from, but I hope he'll use the card if there is something more to him being off. "Let me know what game you want to attend."

"Will do." E.J stares at the card.

"Kid." He looks up at me then. "You really can call me if you need anything. At all."

"Thanks," he says, avoiding my eyes suddenly. Then as the bell rings, he shouts an animated goodbye and heads out of Avery's classroom.

"*That's* more like his usual self." Avery watches the doorway as a few students trickle into the room, a few quickly taking note of my presence. "Thanks for doing that for him."

"It's no problem." I shift on my feet, shoving my hands in my pockets. All poise and class, Avery greets the students before looking back to me. Damn, I don't know what's past *a goner* but that's the level I'm on.

Much like the awkward teenage boys filling the halls, I make the decision to just ask. Could go either way, but hormones and adrenaline leave me little choice but to take another swing. "Can I get your number?"

Her shoulders stiffen, and she glances around the room, I'd guess wondering if any students overheard. "I still don't think it's a good idea," she murmurs quietly.

"Because of history, right?"

She only responds with a nod.

"I have no clue what that even means, Avery," I reach into my wallet, pull out another card, and print my cell number on the back, then slide it across her desk because I don't want to risk her not accepting it from me. "We're on the road for the next week and a half, but you can still use this if you decide you need someone. Because I do know we can't have a history if you won't give us a chance."

I don't wait for a response. Instead, I wave at a few of the students who make eye contact and nod at me before making my way out into the hallway. Damn, she sure is stubborn. But my gut is pretty reliable, and it's telling me there's been some progress made by my impromptu visit today.

Or at least I have to tell myself that. I need to accept how desperate I am for her to give me a chance. It's insane. I've never felt anything close to this before. And that's when I finally realize why I want her to give *me* a chance.

Because she doesn't like baseball. She doesn't like sports.

She met me and wanted nothing to do with Carter Barlowe.

So, if she likes me, it'll be for *me*. Not my fame, not my star status, not my father's legacy. Nothing but the man I am. And for the first time in my life, I'm wondering if I like the man I am without all of those things. I wonder if he's a decent soul, capable of being a whole person. I wonder if Ms. Avery Whitlock, history teacher, didn't just make me question my own history.

11

AVERY

"I can't believe you've left him hanging for a week." Bodie drops his head back on the sofa, rubbing his face. "Avery, he gave you his number a week ago, and you still haven't used it?"

"No, and I don't plan to. I told him I didn't think it was a good idea." But I can't say I wasn't tempted to text him a few times.

The camera zooms in on his face as he removes his hat, glances into it before replacing it snug on his head, then delivers the pitch. Bodie claps after Carter strikes out another batter. It's his third game pitching (ugh—yes, I've been keeping track) and from the looks of it, and the cheers of my best friend, Carter isn't disappointing. I'm less disappointed to watch this game than I care to admit, as well.

"You really need to start watching the games at your place. Or with your brothers. They enjoy all of this stuff." I wave my hand at the screen as the camera stays on Carter, tracking him as he makes his way off the field, down the dugout stairs, to the end of the bench before plopping down.

He gets a few fist bumps, but mostly his teammates leave him alone.

"Are you trying to convince me or yourself?" Bodie snickers.

Grabbing the stack of ungraded pop quizzes off the coffee table, I attempt to focus on them, but my attention keeps getting pulled to the game. The Coyotes capture another win, and the broadcasters talk about Carter for a few seconds before they go to a reporter who's standing with him on the field. I don't even try to pretend I'm not enraptured by that face that has distracted me all week.

"Three down and still on fire," the reporter praises him, running down some stats that mean nothing to me because it's like a foreign language, before asking a few generic questions. He comes across as open and friendly though not chatty; he answers the questions succinctly without seeming like he's brushing her off at all. He's both self-possessed and humble. Aw, hell—I catch myself smiling along with him on the other side of the camera.

I will not swoon.

Then I inwardly cringe and can only imagine what it does to Carter as the reporter asks, "Your dad must be so proud of you. What's he had to say about the season you're having with his team?"

I see it for a split second, the agony in his eyes flashes there and gone before he delivers what I'm sure is a variation of a practiced response. "Oh, yes. So far, the season is going great, but we both know it's a team effort. We both do our best every time we step onto the field. I just want to be the best at my job for those guys."

"Maybe he can introduce us to Cash. That'd be awesome," Bodie suggests.

Yeah. No. Not so much. Even as big of a fan as Bodie is, he doesn't know the truth about Cash, and Carter hides it well. He'd confided in me—which makes me unreasonably happy. Why does that make me feel so good?

The reporter circles back to the subject. *Get a clue, lady*! *He answered your question.* "Are there any plans for your dad to attend a game? Support his club and son in person?"

"Not sure just yet. He's a busy man." Carter shifts on his heels, his arm flexing as he moves slightly back from the reporter, who takes the wrap-up hint. His body language was subtle but effective. *The man does have full command of his body, that's for sure.*

All I want to do is hide away, but Carter doesn't have that luxury—he has to endure these questions day after day, covering his true feeling about Cash. Which makes me wonder why he doesn't just tell the truth, or the very least, refuse to answer questions regarding that part of his life. Is that even an option?

"I should get going. I'm busy the next few days, but please reassure your mom I will make it for Sunday lunch."

"Will do."

"If you get bored, you can come hang out at my place. We're going to do a live podcast for Friday's game."

"I'll pass." Mainly because of the other podcast-mates.

"Since you're not going to use Carter's number, can you kindly hand it over?"

"No! I'm not giving you his phone number so you and your brothers can harass him."

"We wouldn't *harass* him ... just ask a few questions or chat a bit. Maybe," Bodie says as I shake my head. He concedes, walks to the door, and throws it open as I step behind him, ready to shut and lock it after him. He stops abruptly, turning to me. "Do you know what I find really interesting?"

"What's that?" He's going to tell me whether I want to hear it or not.

"That you're holding onto Carter's number even though you have *no intention* of using it." Bodie winks, leaving me to ponder his statement long after he disappears out of sight.

Because it's the truth. I did say (and I meant it) that I have no intention of ever dialing that number. So why hadn't I tossed it in the trash a week ago when he left it on my desk?

12

CARTER

The hot shower does nothing to ease the stiffness in my shoulders. It has nothing to do with my throwing arm and everything to do with the postgame interview, and the possibility of my father attending a game. It's not surprising folks would assume such. Under normal circumstances, within a normal family, it would be expected. But if he shows, I don't want to know about it. Certainly, he's figured that out by now.

Grabbing my phone, I click to find no new messages from him about my game, and unfortunately, no messages from Avery. I know she won't text me, she outright said as much, but it hasn't stopped me from checking my phone more often than usual over the last week.

The team manager calls out through the locker room that it's time to get to the bus. Tomorrow's an off day, but we're heading out tonight for our next road series. Off to the next city where we'll play the day after tomorrow. Traveling's never bothered me before, but I've been ready to get back to Canaan Falls since the moment I boarded the plane. That's definitely an abnormal feeling. And it's irritating as shit.

Fast forward a couple of hours later, and I'm stepping into the hotel room I'll call home for the next few days. The walls feel too tight suddenly, and since tomorrow is a day off, I decide to head down to the hotel bar. One drink won't hurt. I don't indulge often during the season, but I will tonight.

Sliding onto the barstool, I signal the bartender, and order a whiskey neat. He slips the glass across the bar as I do my best to hide my face from the other guests, but I see one who shows recognition. Predictably, she slinks onto the seat beside me.

"Can I buy you a drink?" Her red lips make my stomach turn, and I shift to look straight ahead at the shelves of liquor bottles.

Avery's stubborn face flashes in my mind. I can't envision her ever wearing blood-red lipstick. She's a natural beauty. Her glossy pink lips are what dreams are made of. I shake my head. "I'm good, thanks."

"Are you sure?" She walks her fingers up the outside of my bicep in what I'm positive she thinks is a sexy way, but even with the fabric between her skin and mine, the touch skeeves me out. Legit makes my stomach drop. *Not* in a sexy way.

Shifting away from her, I down the whiskey, eye the bartender, and he refills it pronto. Then I down that one too. So much for one drink. "Yeah. I'm sure."

"Ah. It's a woman that has you all puffed up, because it's not your performance on the field that has you here drinking." When I don't respond, she continues. "I could still help you out. Teach you a few techniques for your off-the-field performance."

I spot Brooks walk in and slide onto a stool at the end of the bar. Turning to Red Lips, I give her as polite a nod as I can muster. "You're not her."

"Hm. Your loss."

Grabbing my refilled glass, I move down the bar to sit next to Brooks.

"Figured you wanted to get to know your new friend a little better." Brooks gestures to Red Lips who has moved on to her next victim across the bar.

"Nope. She's not the one I want to get to know." I laugh darkly, downing the shot. "The one I want to get to know won't give my sorry ass the time of day."

Brooks gives me an encouraging slap on the shoulder. "Good. You needed to eat some humble pie."

"Yeah. Is that what this is called? Because it tastes like hell."

"It's your number one fan, huh? The one who slept through your game."

"She didn't fall asleep until after the game was over," I say with mock outrage. Not that it makes a damn bit of difference. I laugh. "And that was after she finished her book during one of the biggest games of my career. And I'm having the best start to the season ever. But it's not enough anymore."

"Man, she really did get to you." He looks down to his laced fingers as his hands rest on the bar. "I'm sure she'll come around eventually." He waves his hand in my general direction. "This is a lot to take in."

"Thanks. I think." As the bartender approaches to refill my glass, I say, "Can I just get the bottle. Charge it to my tab, and whatever he has."

Brooks waves off the gesture. "Nah. No need for payment —my advice is free of charge. Plus, I think I'll head upstairs too."

"Let's go." I hold the bottle out, feeling the effects as we ride the elevator up to the tenth floor where most of the players are assigned.

As I push my door open (after swiping my key card a few

times) I hear Brooks say my name. When I turn, he's a few feet away. "Are you hoping Cash shows up at a game?"

"Nah. He's a busy man, but I know he supports my career."

"There're no cameras here, Carter."

He's right. There're no cameras around, and I'm still lying to protect the piece of shit who's made my life miserable. Stepping a foot into the room, I give Brooks a nod and let the door shut behind me.

I hold up the bottle as I speak into the empty room. "No. I don't want him at my game because the last time he showed up, I pitched the best game of my Little League career, and he rewarded me by breaking my arm when we got home. Because that was the day he saw me as competition. At the ripe old age of ten, ladies and gentlemen, he feared I'd be a better player than he ever was, and he's hated me every day since."

That's the goddamn answer I should give the reporters, but it's not them who I picture admitting the truth to for the first time. Maybe it's because I've already given some of the truth to her, but I wish Avery was standing in this room with me. I wish she knew the real story. The real person I am and how I became this way.

Bringing the glass to my lips, I take a big gulp before plunking it down on the nightstand and falling across the perfectly made bed, drifting off into a drunken slumber.

13

AVERY

"Ms. W!" E.J. shouts as he slaps the top of the doorframe, entering the classroom. "Where's Carter?"

"Sit down, E.J." I'm glad he's his usual self, but Monday morning is Monday-y enough without being asked about Carter first thing.

"I figured he'd stop by today since he's finally back from the road."

Surprise, surprise: My fingers managed to search up the Coyotes' schedule to see when he'd be back in town. I'm still working to convince myself that it was to have a heads-up on any surprise visits. But I totally know that's not the whole truth. No matter, I won't be informing E.J. of any of the above.

"Carter is a busy guy. I'm sure he's focusing on his work."

"He said he didn't have much going on this week," E.J. says casually. Holy moly. He's really been chatting with Carter. Why does that make me both nervous and relieved that Carter is taking the time to be there for a kid who idolizes him? Hopefully, it doesn't all backfire in our faces.

"Well, *we* have a lot to cover this week, so let's get started."

A few groans sound around the room as I'm already feeling summeritis creeping in. It's still springtime, but the students are already getting antsy for summer break. Can't say that I blame them. Even though I spend my summer at the feed store helping Mom and Dad, it's nice to have a change of pace for a little while, a relaxed routine, and the chance to spend more time with my family.

The class period flies, as does the rest of the day, and Carter is nowhere to be found. Although, while I'm monitoring bus duty, another sports guy appears. Mr. Garcia, the baseball coach, waves to me upon his approach.

"Hey, Avery. How's it going?"

"Good. How about you?" I return his smile, but I'm taken aback a bit by his chipper attitude. Sure, we are colleagues, but other than a grunted hello at our staff in-service days, that's about as far as communication has ever gotten between us.

"Fabulous. Newman mentioned that Carter Barlowe stopped by a few times, and I was wondering if you could ask him to swing by a practice or a game, maybe rally the boys. It's been kind of a bumpy season, and we have a big game coming up."

"Oh, I'm not sure when he'll be around again."

Coach gives me a confused look. "I thought with the signing and everything, he'd be coming around more."

Signing? "Oh, no. He was just touring the school." I'm tempted to offer to give him a call. It's the exact perfect excuse to use that number I can't seem to discard.

"Okay. Well, when you do happen to see him again, maybe put in a word for us. The boys could really use the extra encouragement."

"Sure will." I can definitely agree since I don't know when that might be, and it doesn't require me to seek out Carter.

Coach gives me a warm smile, waving goodbye as he

steps away. E.J. runs past, hurrying to his bus that's already cranked up and about to leave him behind (again) as he shouts, "She's taken, Coach."

Coach gives me a questioning look, but I shake my head at my student. "Get on your bus, Ernest."

E.J. gives me a quick frown but makes it to his bus before the door closes. As I step back, watching the second round of buses depart from school, I see Garcia glance back at me. I'm sure he's confused. I am too.

Once I'm back in my classroom, I notice several missed messages and calls from Dad and Rhett. Quickly clicking Dad's contact, I anxiously wait to hear his voice, dread swirling inside. He's unexpectedly happy when he answers, not troubled at all.

"Hey, Avery. I know you've got your hands full at school, but it's all-hands-on-deck this week." He does a terrible job of covering the speaker before barking instructions meant for somebody else in my ear, but I'm confused as heck.

"'All-hands-on-deck' for what?"

"The signing. I wish you would've given us some warning, but Joe said he'd make sure everything is set up in time, even with the short notice."

"Okay. Who's Joe?" I ask, packing up my things.

"Carter's agent. I figured you'd sent him my way."

Signing ... Coach Garcia said *signing*. And Carter's agent? "Wait. What's going on?"

"I want that side all cleared out and swept," Dad yells before speaking to me again. "I'll see you when you get here, sweetie. Thanks a bunch. Business has already picked up. Love you. Bye."

"Love you too," I reply just in time to hear the line go silent. Quickly grabbing my stuff, I head straight to the store just outside of town. On the ride over, I try to reach both of my sisters and my brother, then dial Mom. No one is answering their phone, and once I arrive, I understand why. When Dad said all-hands-on-deck, he meant it. Even Finn is running around with a push broom. Although making little headway, he's still attempting to help.

Dad greets me then calls out, "Mom needs you to help her in the breakroom."

"What's going on?" I ask as Dad continues his task, but Rhett looks to me.

"Your boy has everyone running around like they're insane," Rhett says. "How'd you convince him to do it here?"

"Do what?" My voice rises as I ask. "What the hell is happening?"

A few customers look my way as Rhett grabs my elbow and pulls me aside. "Did he really not tell you?"

"Does it look like I'm in the know?"

"No, but that's not unusual for you," Rhett jokes. "Carter is having a fan signing here at the store on Thursday evening. And he's Dad's new favorite child, by the way."

"A signing. Why would he do that?"

"I don't know. But he's really rolling out the red carpet for it. They're sending some fancy caterer over and said they'd have someone come by tomorrow to help clean up, but Dad insisted we start getting everything ready tonight since it's already been announced." Rhett motions to the crowd walking around the store.

It's always had its fair share of business, but from the looks of it, a bigger crowd has definitely descended. And I should be thankful. "I wonder why he didn't tell me?"

"Probably because you would've refused him. Again," Bodie says from behind me.

I jump, not realizing he was even here at all. "Did you know what he was up to?"

"Nope. Not until your dad called and asked if I could bring my brothers over to help."

Great. "Why on earth would he schedule a signing at a feed store of all places?"

"If you *really* don't know the answer to that question then you're even more clueless than I thought." Bodie snickers as he steps away, resuming his task. It's then that I spot my least favorite of his brothers. I can't believe he has the nerve to show up here. At all.

Hurrying to the back, I find Mom straightening out the cabinets as Presley organizes the table and chairs, taking note of my arrival. "About time the princess arrived."

Normally her jabs don't bother me, but I'm in no mood. "Yeah. I would've been here much earlier had I known anything about it."

"Oh, it's no problem, sweetie. Just help me get all this straight." Mom opens another cabinet, hurriedly organizing the plastic cups.

"I doubt he'll look through the cabinets, Mom." Presley rolls her eyes as she slams a chair against the table.

"The place has needed a good spring cleaning, so this is the perfect reason for it." Mom looks to Presley. "So cut the attitude."

Mom has a sweet voice, but we all know she means business—even if we are grown and out of the house. Presley doesn't seem to receive the message as she huffs and stomps out of the room.

Mom says, "She'll come around."

"Yeah. That makes one of us." Because my head is still spinning with more questions than answers as I help Mom. I know Bodie was implying Carter had set this up here because of me, but that still doesn't make any sense. A quick stop by the school with coffee was expected. Involving my family in his insidious mission? Didn't see that one coming. Just when I thought I was prepared for his next play, Carter Barlowe throws me a curveball.

14

CARTER

Another game down. Another day closer to my start in the rotation. I don't mind sitting in the dugout and supporting my teammates, but I want to be in the mix; I was made for the action, not watching from the bench.

I'm just about to head out of the clubhouse when I feel my phone vibrate in my jeans pocket. Pulling it out, I read the text a few times.

Unknown: The pointless and boring game has been over long enough. Get your ass out here now.

I stare at the message and hope it's the one person I've been waiting on to message me—although this wasn't exactly the type of vibe I'd hoped to receive.

Me: On my way.

Unknown: Thanks, asshat.

I chuckle, knowing it's her. No one else would call me an asshat and demand anything from me. They'd kiss my ass and ask for instructions on what to do next.

Sure enough, when I step outside and look to the edge of the player's parking, where our lot meets the public access area, I'm met with Avery's angry glare. I make my way to her, then open the gate for her to step into the restricted area. Her hair is a mess. Her clothes are dusty. She's never looked more beautiful, and I have to smile at her frustration as she zones in on me.

"What's going on?" I ask to her further dismay.

"That was my very question earlier this evening. And of all the ways I could have spent the remainder of my Monday, cleaning up my parents' store for a damn event that I had no clue was even happening was *nowhere* on my list."

"I should've—"

"No, you shouldn't have *anything*." Her frustration morphs into full-blown anger as she squares up to me. "You can mess with my job, screw around with my feelings, but the moment you start jacking with my family, you've crossed the line."

Ouch. She's *mad* mad. "I'm not *jacking* with your family. And it wasn't my intention to mess with your job or screw with your feelings, although I'm glad to know I've had *some* effect on the latter." God knows she's twisted mine all to hell. I'm so clearly screwed up, some random woman in a bar called me out on it. Jesus.

"Why would you schedule a signing at a feed store—my parents' location, of all places?"

Joe thought it was a little off too, but he didn't question it for a second as he was relieved that I was finally willing to agree to the event voluntarily after he'd been asking to schedule for the last few months. "Local businesses benefit from the publicity, and your dad seemed to be happy about it."

"Yes, because he doesn't know it's only all about the challenge for you." She moves to walk around me, but I step in front of her, backing her into the wall as she stares up to me.

"My only challenge is getting those hazel eyes out of my mind." She remains silent, so I seize the opportunity to explain. "Despite your low opinion of me, I wouldn't do anything to hurt your parents' business. It's an event that we'll mutually benefit from. I'll provide everything needed. It won't cost your parents anything and should bring in more customers. It's a win-win." Except maybe it's not. Maybe I'll never win with her. Because nothing I do in her eyes doesn't have hidden motives.

"My parents built that store from the ground up. If you do anything to sabotage them, I will hurt you."

I have no doubt that she could. Deeply. "You won't have to. My intentions are honorable, even if their daughter thinks the worst of me."

"She doesn't know what to think." Her voice fades out as she tilts her face away from me, and I step back.

"Night, Lowe. Night, Avery," Brooks calls, giving us a friendly wave as he grins. I'm guessing his view of the situation is skewed because this isn't a good visit like I'd hoped for when he was giving my drunk ass a pep talk the other night.

Her guard is immediately back up and fastening securely in place. "Who is that and how the hell does he know my name?"

"Brooks. Third baseman." Damn good advice giver just needs a better execution. "Do you want to grab a bite to eat or something?"

She quickly shakes her head, moving to make her usual escape. "It's late, and I have to be at work early."

Silently, I watch as she hurries back into the empty public parking lot before hopping into a black Ford truck and speeding off.

Grabbing my phone, I shoot off a quick message.

Me: Please make sure everything goes smoothly Thursday. It's important that it does.

Joe: Got it. All you have to do is show up. Don't worry.

Usually that would be the case, but I've already confirmed

with Avery's dad that I'll be there early on Thursday to help set up.

Walking to my truck, I drop into the driver's seat and commute the few miles to my house. Stepping inside the kitchen, I'm met with silence. What must it have been like to grow up with a house full of siblings and parents who were actually around?

Grabbing my phone out of my pocket, I add her number as a contact, thankful to have a connection to her, even if she does hate me at the moment. I risk the fact that she might respond to my text by calling me another choice name, but I type in the message anyway.

Me: Good night, Avery.

Three dots indicate she's typing for several seconds before the message finally comes through.

Avery: Night, Carter.

I'm guessing it wasn't the original message she typed out, but I log it as a W tonight.

15

AVERY

Fortunately, today's lesson doesn't require much teaching and instead relies heavily on quiet work because I'm exhausted both mentally and physically. Even after going home last night, it took me forever to fall asleep because my mind was racing from the latest development with Carter Barlowe and the circus he calls a life.

Dad has already sent some excited morning texts outlining specific instructions for his plans around the store this evening and Thursday morning. This is a make-or-break moment for Carter, because if he is messing with my parents' livelihood in the name of capturing my attention, it will tell me more about him than anything else ever will. But deep down, I don't believe he would do that. Besides, he's gotten my full attention at this point. But I can't quite let my guard down just yet. When my phone vibrates, I wonder if he knew I was thinking of him.

Carter: Good morning, beautiful.

How the heck do I respond to that? I'd hate to admit (to myself as much as him) that it makes me happy to hear from him—just like the good night message had last night. So, I decide snark is my best defense.

Me: Is that what you tell yourself in the mirror?

I bite back a smile, imagining him checking himself out in the mirror.

Carter: Only when I need an extra boost to get through the day after I'm turned down by a gorgeous woman.

Me: I'm sure you'll recover soon enough.

Carter: Doubt it.

I don't respond, but Carter doesn't waste any time sending another message.

Carter: E.J. says you look extra tired today.

Looking up, I find E.J. focusing on his assignment before he looks to me. A half-smile breaks across his face, and I somehow know he's aware that he's been caught crossing enemy lines. Little traitor.

Me: Yeah. Someone decided to spring a big event on my family at the last minute.

Carter: Lyle said everything was under control, but the crew will be there today to help out. I'll be there all day Thursday to make sure the whole shebang goes smoothly. Start to finish.

Lyle? He's on first name basis with my dad. Fantastic. This is going to be more disastrous than I first thought.

Me: I'll be there too.

I make a note to put in for a personal day on Thursday. It's last minute, but I haven't taken many this year, none this semester, in fact, but the thought of Carter running around with my parents all day has me more on edge than missing a day of work.

Carter: It's a date.

Me: No. It's not.

Carter: Third date to be exact.

Me: Not a date, and definitely not a third one.

Carter: Coffee was first date.

Me: No, it wasn't, but that still doesn't make it the third date.

Carter: Two coffee dates does, though. Three creams and two sugars. Any pastries, croissants, donuts? Fruit? You didn't eat anything last time, so I don't know what you like.

I'd *like* a reality check. How, how, how does Carter paying enough attention to know how I take my coffee make me giddy?

Me: Never agreed to a first or second coffee date.

Carter: It's the least I can do since E.J. said you look like you could really use some coffee today, and it's kinda my fault with the signing and everything.

Me: Yeah. It is your fault. No "kinda" about it.

Carter: See you second period.

I'm in trouble. Messaging him had been a rash decision last night because I'd been waiting outside the stadium for a good half hour. After watching several players and staff leave, it was easy to be pissed even more at him, so I sent him the text as a means to make myself feel better. I wanted to see him in person, tell him not to mess with my parents to his absurdly handsome face, and then I'd stupidly admitted he's screwing with my feelings.

It may very well have been dumb to say it aloud, but I'm aware he clearly is because I keep glancing at the door until the second period bell rings. And then he appears right on time, two coffees in hand along with a paper sack. And as much as I need the coffee, I'm excited to see the person holding the beverages.

He passes me one of the paper cups, leaning over as he says, "E.J. was wrong. You look extra gorgeous today." Stepping back, he pulls up a chair, casually taking a seat as he sips from his matching cup.

I take it back.

I'm not in trouble.

I'm wholly, completely, utterly screwed.

16

CARTER

She fumbles around with some notebooks on her desk before finally relaxing and enjoying her coffee. But she's still avoiding looking my way. But she's not telling me to leave. After her reaction last night to the signing news, I really thought I'd messed it all up. But maybe things can work out after all. Brooks will be happy to hear it.

"Why don't you come to the game tonight?"

Shock crosses her face before it's masked with annoyance. "I have plans to clean up a feed store tonight thanks to someone."

"The crew should be there helping, so I'm sure they can spare you for a few hours." Because I really want her at the game.

"It *would* be a good time to catch up on my sleep, I need a few extra z's." She grins as she lifts the cups to her lips to take a sip. "But I already told my dad I'd help out tonight."

"Then I'll meet you there after the game."

"We'll probably be done before that. I mean … gosh, I hope so, anyway."

"Then let me take you out on a real date tonight."

She remains silent for a second before saying, "But I thought we're already set for the third date."

"I definitely think this calls for a fourth date on Thursday with the third one tonight."

"I have class in the morning. And don't you have to practice or something?"

"Then I guess we'll have to squeeze in some more coffee dates until this weekend when you don't have an early class."

She shifts uncomfortably. "Aren't you starting tonight?"

The fact that she knows that makes me happier than it should. "Yep."

"You should probably be focusing on that, then. Oh, speaking of focusing, Coach Garcia asked if you could give his players a quick word of encouragement. Apparently, it's been a rough season for the team."

"I can handle that. And my attention is focused exactly where it needs to be." My season is going excellent—I'm three for three—and I'm finally making some progress with the stunning woman in front of me. I can't describe what it feels like for her to actually see me for me, to take me at face value without factoring in all the other added bullshit. It's an astounding experience.

She shifts, a slight bit of unease as she masks it with what I've learned is her go-to defense of sarcasm. "You sure are certain of yourself, as usual."

On the field, yes. "Hard work and determination haven't let me down yet."

"Hardheadedness is more like it."

"*You* have no room to talk, Ms. W." I smile at her eye roll, an annoyed acknowledgement of defeat. "But I do need you to tell me one very important detail." Her unease grows a bit before I ask, "Danish, croissant, fruit, or muffin?"

"Muffin."

"Blueberry, banana nut, or chocolate chip?"

"How much did you buy, Carter?"

"A few options." One of everything in the coffee shop.

"Banana nut."

Reaching into the paper sack, I grab out her muffin of choice, thankful to finally know something she likes even if it is something as simple as the baked good I'm handing to her.

She leans back in her chair, finally relaxing as she takes a bite. I can't look away from her mouth. I want to taste her more than any sweet treat in that bag.

"What's your pick?" she asks, motioning to the pastries.

You. "I'm a sucker for sweets. I have to limit myself so I don't go overboard."

"Don't dare say that to my mom. She'll see it as her mission to bake everything under the sun for you." The way her face lights up when she talks about her family makes me crave that feeling more than any food craving I've ever felt.

"She sounds wonderful. Your dad is too." I didn't talk to him for long but between the conversation and the magnificent woman they raised in front of me, I know they're everything I'd ever want for a parent. "The business he built from a summer lawn-mowing job is nothing short of extraordinary."

My dad was born into money. He never worked a day in his life, immediately gliding from high school to his career in the big leagues, bypassing higher education because he never needed a backup plan. He knew he could rely on his father's wealth to bail him out. My father's wealth was the last thing I wanted, even making a point to pay for my higher education on my own after refusing a scholarship that I wasn't certain was offered to me for my abilities.

"My dad is the best. Which is why it's important to me that everything goes well, for his sake and my mom's. And yours." She gives me a joking side-eye, but I see the worry shining through her smile. And I don't blame her. The people in her life are special to her, and she wants to keep them safe.

"It will. And so will our date afterwards." I give her a wink, knowing I will do absolutely everything in my power to make sure both go off without a hitch.

"We'll see." She brings the coffee cup up to her smirking lips, taking a sip.

She didn't refuse me, so it's definitely a swing and a hit. I've never been so damn thrilled over a date as I am about her not turning me down flat again for a date. So, I let the topic drop as I listen to her speak about her family. The more she talks, the more I'm looking forward to spending the day with all of them, her especially, because our current coffee date is over way too fast for my liking.

"Well, my students will be along in about five minutes." She glances at her phone before shuffling items around on her tidy desk.

Reaching over, I tenderly grab her hand in mine, rubbing my thumb along her wrist as I lift her knuckles to my mouth, feathering a gentle kiss across them. "Let me know if you change your mind about tonight."

I stand, moving the chair back to its place. "I'll find the coach and tell him you sent me to rally his team." I regretfully turn to leave the classroom and seek out the damn coach when I'd rather park my ass in this classroom or anywhere she is, really.

"Carter," she says softly. When I turn, she's got the most magnificent smile on her face. "Thank you."

"My pleasure." And damn it, it is. The only thing I can think as I make my way through the high school is I hope it's the first of many days where we're on good terms. And I really hope I'm done watching her bail on me.

17

AVERY

The morning has been perfect. Surreal, but perfect. Introducing Carter to my dad face-to-face was a bizarre moment. Even though Dad is a fan, he never showed it. Instead, he started bossing Carter around just like he does the rest of us, and Carter fell right into line. In fact, Carter fits in with us almost too perfectly as we move around the store and wrap up some last-minute things that Dad wanted done before the signing tonight. And I have to say, the store hasn't looked this good in years, if ever—we've wiped every square inch of it down. And Carter is still at it, putting in the work with Rhett to finish up their latest task.

"So, what's the deal with y'all?" Presley asks, startling me. But it's a good thing she jolted me out of my reverie, as I realize now I'd just been standing staring at Carter. Again.

"There's no deal. He wanted to help out Mom and Dad's business."

"Yeah. Sure, Avery." My little sister all but undresses him with her eyes, making me want to fist fight her for the first time since we were kids. "Then you won't mind if I go over and thank him properly for everything he's doing for our parents." Her suggestive smirk tells me what her idea of "properly" entails.

"Stay away from him, Presley."

"Why, sis? There's nothing going on between the two of you, right?" she goads. "I can't wait to see under that T-shirt." She moves to walk over, but I step in front of her.

"Stop it."

"Not until you admit it." Her patronizing smirk tells me she wants the intel, not for my benefit, but to use to hers however she might decide during her next bratty episode.

"Admit what?" Tessa asks, walking in at the perfect time from picking Finn up from his day school. It doesn't take her long to assess what she's walked into. "If y'all act crazy, Dad is gonna be in a bad mood the rest of the day. This is too important of a day for him and Mom. And Carter," she says looking to me.

Finn runs into my side, bear-hugging me with his little arms. I reach down and pluck him up, settling him on my hip and wrapping the welcome interruption in a warm hug as I try to shake off my frustration with Presley. It doesn't take long for the feeling to recede as Finn wraps his arms around my neck. "I missed you, buddy."

"Me too." He places a wet smooch on my cheek as Carter walks up to us.

"Carter, this is Finn, my nephew. Finn, this is my friend Carter."

Carter extends his hand as Finn gives him a weary look before accepting it. He wiggles, so I set him down, and he's off to Tessa who asks if he wants to go with her to our parents' house or stay at the store with his granny. He opts to go to Granny's for a snack, and it sounds like a plan.

"I'm a mess." I rub my hands over my yoga pants, pulling my T-shirt away. So much for keeping myself halfway decent looking, not that it should matter. "I'm gonna head to my parents' house to get ready." It's more convenient since it's just a short walk from the store and much closer than my place.

"Mind if I tag along?" Carter asks, waving a hand over his just-as-messy appearance. "I could use some freshening up too, so Joe doesn't lecture me."

"Sure." I tell Dad we'll be right back, and Carter and I head outside. He grabs a bag from his truck, and I do the same. As we walk in silence, I cull my mind for topics of conversation. Something. Anything. But all I can think about is showering at my parents' house with Carter there. And him doing the same as my mind instantly visualizes what's beneath the T-shirt that I've watched cling to his body every damn time he moved in a way that made his muscles more than noticeable.

Stop it, Avery. I shake the thoughts out of my head, looking ahead. Tessa and Finn are way ahead of us, disappearing through the front door as we continue the walk to the house tucked behind the store.

"Is this where you grew up?" Carter breaks the silence. Thank you, baby Jesus.

"Yep."

"It must've been nice growing up here with such a big family."

"Yes. It really was." I smile.

"Now I know why you were so quick to protect your family. They're awesome. Your dad especially." There's sincerity in his voice, but I sense pain in it too. And it makes me grateful for the family and parents I was lucky enough to be born to, because from the little I know, Carter didn't get dealt a good hand from the parent deck.

"Can I ask you a personal question?"

"Of course," he responds too quickly.

"About your dad." I add to make sure he really is okay

with it. Today has been wonderful but the question keeps playing in my mind.

"Ask me anything, Avery."

"Why don't you tell the truth when they ask you about him?" We take another few steps and he doesn't say anything, so I add something I'm a bit embarrassed to admit. "I saw your interview after one of the games. And I was curious about it." I wave a hand in the air. "But you don't have to answer. Sorry."

He stops, looking to the ground as I halt beside him, afraid I've overstepped until his expression softens. He wasn't avoiding the question, it appears he's thoughtfully composing an answer. "Because the media will spin it one of two ways: I'll either be the bitter child trying to ruin my father's legacy in the sport or a pity story where I'm the victim. And neither are narratives I want to take part in. I'm not covering for him or lying for him. I've chosen to take control of the story so I don't have to play a part in someone else's commentary on it. I'm entirely uninterested in partici-pating in any version of an exposed 'he said, he said' type of scenario with him. If the media gets wind that there's a story behind the scenes, it will play out in a very public way, and it won't ever end. This way, the focus stays on the game. And not him."

"That makes sense." It does. But I can't help but feel sorry for him and it confirms exactly what he's saying.

"Don't," he says, clasping my hand in his as we continue walking. "Don't look at me like that."

"Like what?" I ask, already knowing what he's about to say.

"I told you about him because I trust you. I want you to understand me, not pity me."

"Thank you for telling me." We approach the house, step inside, and I see Carter take a look around.

"The bathroom is straight through there." I point down the hallway. "You go first because I have a snack date." Finn runs into the room as if on cue and grabs my finger to illustrate my point, pulling me to the kitchen.

"First a book, then a nap, now a snack date. I can't compete with that one for sure." Carter grabs his chest, acting like he's defeated before grinning.

He has to know he's not only competing but kicking ass on capturing my attention as he stands in my childhood home, looking hella enticing even covered in sweat and dirt. "Don't be a buttface."

Carter laughs at Finn's favorite "bad word." My nephew isn't supposed to be saying it, so I probably shouldn't either because he giggles and repeats me, causing Carter's smile to grow.

"Chop, chop," I instruct Carter. Following instructions, he walks down the hallway.

In the kitchen with Finn, we sit at the table and dig into some fruit and sandwiches that Mom had prepared ahead of time, knowing we'd all end up at the house to snack before the big event tonight.

When Carter exits the bathroom after his shower looking too damn good, I hurriedly distract myself before I say or do something stupid. Playing up my hostess role, I tell him to help himself to some food or have a seat in the living room, and I'll get cleaned up quickly and be right out.

Once in the small bathroom, I take a deep breath and look in the mirror. That stupid little voice inside me still wonders if I'm only a challenge for now. Will he get bored with me after I completely give in? My gut tells me no, but does a fool know when they're being a fool? My gut also says no. Attempting to hush the voice, I step into the shower and hurry to rinse off. Ten minutes and a hot shower later, I emerge feeling like a new person.

Rounding the corner into the living room, I'm struck by an unexpected sight. Carter is sitting on the sofa, his head leaned back against the cushion, sound asleep. It looks like I'm not the only one who falls asleep easily. We have been at it since 5 a.m., though, and I know I could use a nap too, so it's hard to blame the guy.

"We're heading back to the front, Ave," Tessa yells. "Finn, let's go! Shake a leg!"

Carter startles at Tessa's holler and luckily doesn't catch me staring at him. Thankfully, no camera was around to capture the role reversal. As he sits forward, and I take a closer look at him, all the words I've ever known leave my mind as my hand clasps over my mouth.

He did not.

"What is it?" Carter asks, his tone of voice drawing Tessa's attention. Her eyes widen as she stares in shock at the sight too.

"Finn," Tessa shouts. "In here. Now!"

"Avery, what's wrong?" Carter's concern only grows a smidgen as mine increases by the second.

"Finn, what on earth?" Tessa scolds the innocent-looking but definitely responsible child as she points to Carter, who still looks baffled.

"Aunt Avery told me to do it."

"No I did not!" I shout as Carter stands, looking between us like we're all crazy.

"You said buttfaces should come with a warning on their head." He literally squints and crosses his arms. Full of right-eous confidence that he followed my directions to the letter. No remorse, the kid is utterly aloof.

Shit. "I-I-I … I did. I did say that to Rhett," I raise my eyebrows at Finn. "But I wasn't serious."

Finn coolly shrugs. "Oops."

"Finn! You should know better!" Tessa fusses.

With my hands on my cheeks, I say, "Should he? Should we expect him to be aware of the nuances of sarcasm?"

Carter walks to the mirror over the fireplace and leans closer to read the word *buttface* written across his forehead in Sharpie.

"In this family? Maybe! Seriously, Avery. Why would you say that?" Tessa asks.

Carter turns to face me, pointing to his forehead. "You told him to do this to me?"

"No, not to you *exactly* …." I attempt to bite back a laugh but fail when a smile moves across Carter's lips, and he shakes his head. "On the bright side, his handwriting is getting better. Very legible," I tease my sister.

"Who else did you do this to?" Tessa asks Finn, not finding any of this the least bit funny.

"Uncle Rhett, but it was on his arm." I thought that would be an excellent place to end his explanation. But my darling Finn did not agree. "Then Aunt Avery said *buttface* should've been written across his forehead to give anyone who looks at him twice a fair warning." He shrugs.

"Well, thank you, court reporter, for reading the transcript back to the room. What, do you have a photographic memory I wasn't aware of? Sheesh." I give my sister a *yikes* face, then say, "Things we've learned today: his handwriting has improved, he's a keen listener, and he's got perfect recall. You've got a special kid on your hands, here."

"Carter, I'm sorry." Tessa looks to her son. "Apologize, Finn."

Finn gives Carter a sheepish look. "Sorry, Mr. Carter."

"It's no prob, buddy. But next time, it's Aunt Avery's turn."

Tessa shakes her head. "Can y'all please stop giving him ideas?"

"Come on," I say to Carter. "Rubbing alcohol will take it right off."

Tessa and Finn walk out of the house as I lead Carter back down the hallway to the bathroom. Instructing him to sit on the vanity chair, I then grab some cotton balls and rubbing alcohol. "I really am sorry. I said that a couple weeks ago to my brother—I don't remember Finn even being in the room." I dab the cotton against his forehead as I try to avoid gazing directly into his alluring eyes because I can see him looking up at me as I lean over him, acutely aware of how close my chest is to his face.

"Your declaration of remorse would be a lot more convincing if you weren't laughing as you said it."

"Well in my defense, you *can* be a buttface sometimes." My laugh is cut off this time when Carter's firm hands grip my hips and pull me down to him. I end up on his lap as he guides me to straddle him while his fingers twine into the hair at the nape of my neck. Gripping my hair lightly, he crashes his mouth to mine, devouring me in a kiss that causes every sensible thought I've ever had to leave my mind.

Gripping his shoulders, I cling to him as his hands slip under my shirt, gliding up the bare skin of my back as he presses me closer to him. And I want to feel more of him, which somehow snaps me out of the lusty fog. I pull back, ending the kiss but taking a moment before opening my eyes to look at him. When I do, need is apparent in his eyes, and I wonder if he sees it in mine as well. Gently tucking my hair behind my ear with his big strong hand, I know he understands I need to slow it down. It's too much too fast. He's too much.

His palm cups my cheek, his thumb strokes my skin delicately, and he leans forward, feathering a tender kiss on my lips before shifting back. Without a word, I stand, grabbing the cotton ball and swabbing the ink off his skin. My cheeks flush under his heated gaze; I'm more than aware of how he's watching me.

I move away, feeling exposed, like he's looking straight through me. I've never felt so vulnerable. I toss the cotton in the trash and turn to walk out of the bathroom. "All done."

His hand lightly grips my arm, and I turn back to him. In a surprisingly strained tone, he says, "Are we okay, Avery?"

"Yes, we're good. But we really should get back to the store. It's almost time for the signing to start." I walk out of the house as he quietly follows behind me. I'm internally wigging out, and somehow, I think he knows it, but is giving me room to handle it. *It was just a stupid kiss, so there's no point in making a big deal out of it. It's not a big deal.* Ugh, why does that bother me?

Glancing toward the store, I see the crowd already gathering to meet the famous Carter Barlowe. *Remember the real reason he's here right now, Avery.* No matter his intentions, this will be a great thing for my parents. "Wow. I don't think the parking lot has ever been this packed before."

"Avery," Carter says, as I turn a forced smile on him. "Do you want to grab some supper after the crowd clears out?"

"That'll probably be awhile from the looks of it," I deflect with a smile, but he won't let me off that easy.

"Joe will have everyone in and out in a timely and orderly fashion, like he always does at these things. And if you're done running away from me, I'd love to grab a bite to eat."

He just called me out, and all I can think is he really can be a buttface sometimes, but so can I. There's no good reason for me to question his motives, but I still am. Stopping, I turn to face him. "Why? Why me? Is it all about the challenge, Carter? Because if it is, you have to know you've already accomplished your goal."

His sexy grin pisses me off as he tilts his head, looking to the ground.

As I turn to hurry away, he wraps an arm around my lower back, his lips near mine. I think he's going to kiss me again but instead says, "You asked a question that I'd really like to answer. Avery,"—he says my name almost reverently and I see *something* in his eyes; something profound in its truth and honesty—"you're so much more than a challenge. When I realized that you hate baseball, that you couldn't give two shits who Carter or Cash Barlowe are, I knew if you ever wanted me, it'd be solely for *me*. Nothing else. No hidden agenda. No secret motives." With that, he tenderly feathers a kiss over my lips. "Just me for me."

The fact that Carter lives his life questioning people's intentions on the daily makes me understand him in a whole new way. He has his own reasons to worry about being someone else's conquest—it's different for him but no less hurtful. That *something* in his deep-brown eyes moves me. Convinces me in its sincerity that he's not bullshitting me in the least. These are not lines he'd say to any random fame chaser looking to hook up. Of that, I'm sure. "You're still a buttface."

He laughs at my jab, intertwining his fingers in mine. "Then have supper with me so I can make it up to you."

"I'll think about it."

But we both know the answer already.

CARTER

"What are you in the mood for?" Avery still looks a little nervous as she sits in the passenger seat of my truck, but at least she's here with me. I'll eat any damn thing she wants.

"Doesn't matter. What are you in the mood for?"

You. But I keep that response to myself so she doesn't completely hide away from me. "There's a good steak house nearby."

"Sounds good."

At the restaurant, only one couple recognizes me, but they don't approach. Not many do in general, but it's something I'm definitely hoping to avoid on my first official date with Avery. We're seated quickly and I don't miss the way she glances around the restaurant.

"Is it always like that?" Avery asks as I watch her.

"Like what?"

"I don't know. Smiling and answering the same questions over and over."

"Pretty much."

"Thanks again for doing it at the store. Dad is still on cloud nine. But I think it's more because he has new customers to get to know now." She smiles. "He makes a point to know every customer by name and what they purchase when they come in. Presley once suggested that we assign numbers to the customer roster and Dad completely lost it. You'd have thought she'd suggested throwing their names in the burn pile. He's always said the personal touch is what brings them back to the store."

"So, did you work there growing up?"

"Yep. Still do during summer break. I actually enjoy it. I love getting to spend that time with family—except for Rhett, he tends to drive everyone crazy." She laughs as she speaks of her younger brother.

"Yeah. He seems like a character, much like his nephew." I point to my forehead. "Is he always so fearless?"

"Yep. Tessa complains, says we all spoil him, but it's hard not to."

"I can understand why."

We fall into an easy conversation, talking about her family mostly, although it does move to mine occasionally, and I'm able to answer with ease. It's never been this comfortable and effortless with anyone. Or maybe I never cared to put the energy in before since I'd always questioned their motives. And now that I know what she's had in her mind, it makes sense why she'd been standoffish before. Although, I can still sense that she has one eye on me, and one constantly glancing over her shoulder, watching for a runner to steal a base while trying to keep focused on the pitch being delivered to the person at the plate. I won't aim for the stands. I'll bunt, keep the ball in play until she's able to recognize the only game I'm playing is the one where catching and keeping her makes me the winner. And it's a good decision, the meal goes well.

Afterwards, as we walk to my truck, I decide (against my

better judgment) to say what I'm thinking aloud. "I know it's late, but I'm not ready for the night to end."

And I'm freakin' ecstatic when she responds, "Me neither."

"Do you want to go somewhere or back to your place or mine?" I tried to make my innocent suggestion obvious but the statement is loaded with assumptions, so I clarify, "No expectations. I just want to hang out a little longer. We can watch a movie or whatever."

"Okay." She agrees, but I sense her reluctance.

We decide on my place, and once I pull in the driveway, I feel her unease notch up.

"Avery, let me know when you're ready to call it a night, even if it's now."

"I'm not ready yet." She gives me a reassuring smile that doesn't put my mind to rest. But at least she's not running.

Leading her into the house, we step into the kitchen, and I grab a bottle of water for her. As she accepts it, she stares at me for the first time like I'm a stranger. I immediately miss the familiarity in her eyes, there's a hint of darkness, and it nearly makes my stomach turn to think I'll lose that light I've come to crave when I look into her hazel eyes.

Stepping in front of her, her hip leans against the counter as I prop my hands on the stone countertop on either side of her, searching her eyes. "What are you thinking?"

"It's just ... more than I was expecting." Her eyes dart over my shoulder. "I mean, my entire apartment fits in your kitchen."

"Don't. Don't do that."

"Do what?"

"Look at me differently, like everyone else does. All it is is a big empty house that my agent picked out for me. I didn't want to move back to this town, so I had zero desire to house shop."

"Why wouldn't you want to pick out a place for yourself once you signed with the team?"

"Because I didn't plan on staying here." Shock is evident on her face, and I say something I may regret later, but she needs to hear it. "But plans change."

Leaning forward, I tenderly brush my lips over hers, waiting for her response. When she kisses me back, I dive deeper into it, savoring her every second she allows me to do so. She's here. She's letting me in. And I can't get enough of her, relishing in her as long as she'll allow. When she breaks the contact, I clasp her hand in mine and lead her to the media room that I've only used to study game reels since moving in.

Passing her the remote, I say, "Pick any movie. I'll be right back."

Making my way down the hallway, I step into the bathroom and take a second. Pressing my palms against the cold marble countertop, my head hangs down as I utter, "Don't fuck this up." Because it's not the town or this house or even the team that makes it feel like home, it's her. And that scares the shit out of me. The town my father lives in was supposed to be a pit stop, not the place I hang my hat.

19

AVERY

Sitting on the couch—*Carter's couch*—I glance around before flipping through the movie selections and choosing a comedy. A few minutes go by before he joins me on the couch, sitting a few feet away. *Alright, you're letting me know this is not a* Netflix-and-chill *situation. Message received.*

Something is off with him, but I'm not sure if I'm imagining it or if it's simply the fact that's we're both adjusting to whatever is happening between us. After a few minutes, he shifts closer, so I tuck my feet up under me, enjoying when he drapes his arm around my shoulders. I lean against him, failing to focus on the movie. Instead, I study the shelves beside the TV, noting they're filled with only décor, no pictures. It's not Carter Barlowe, star pitcher of the Coyotes, represented within these walls. It's the kid who probably grew up in a home just as grand and uninviting as this one. Money sure didn't buy the Barlowe family happiness, and though I don't pity Carter, that fact does make my heart sad for the kid he used to be and the man he is today. He deserved to grow up in a home full of laughter and happy memories; a home where there wasn't enough wall space to display all the favorite family photos.

Nuzzling closer to him, I let out a contented sigh. Being in Carter's embrace is cozy; I fit into the nook he's created for me perfectly. He still smells fresh from the shower he'd taken earlier at my parents' house, and a little thrill shoots through me when I inhale that familiar scent on him. I'm still enjoying his warmth and being nestled against him when my alarm sounds on my cell phone.

The one that wakes me up for work.

My hands press against a solid chest as I look down. I realize that I must have fallen asleep on Carter's couch ... or rather *on* Carter. He stirs a bit, and the arm he's had snaked around my lower back pulls me to him. He's sleeping too—snuggling closer in his sleep, no less—but my palms press against this chest, and I quickly jump off him, shutting off my alarm.

"I have to go. I'm gonna be late for work." How did this happen? I just closed my eyes for a few seconds, and ... Isn't that how every story that ends in calamity starts? *I don't know what happened, but ... blah, blah, blah.* Ugh.

"I'll drive you." Carter stretches and yawns, calmly rising off the couch. Apparently, he's not sharing in my panic.

"I can't be late." Translation: Move your ass. "My truck is still at my parents' store." Oh no. They'll realize I didn't pick it up last night after leaving with Carter. It's not like it's a big deal, but some people (named Rhett) will make a big deal about it. "Great."

"Avery, it's okay, I don't need to drive you, just take my truck. We can get yours later. That way you won't be late."

"Take your truck?"

"Yeah. I'll use one of my other vehicles today."

"Other vehicles?" He says it like we're discussing me

borrowing a spare pair of socks or something. "How many vehicles do you have?"

The grogginess is gone from his face as he flatly replies, "Four."

"Okay." Wow. Four vehicles for one person.

"I'll swing by during your free period with some coffee."

"You don't have to." I turn away from him as I hunt for my shoes.

"Avery." His soft tone causes me to hesitate before looking to him. He extends his hand, dropping his key fob into my palm, and gives me a quick kiss on my cheek. "I'll see you in a few hours."

I clutch the key fob in my hand, grab my purse, and bolt from the media room. Once in the garage, I click a few buttons before I finally open the correct garage bay and back the truck out. Only now noting one other vehicle, and guessing he probably has some secret Batcave with the other two.

Damn it. Why can't I act normal around him? *What is normal anymore?* There're times when I'm with him that I forget all the other bullshit of who he is and what he does. But then there are other times where, whether he wants to accept it or not, he is *the* Carter Barlowe. And I'm not sure how to wrap my head around the entire situation. It's even more evident as I drive his fancy truck across town to my place, get dressed in record time, then hightail it to school, arriving just in time.

I'm flustered (obviously) and attempting to get settled at my desk when I hear a familiar whoop and slap on the door-frame. I don't look up until I hear E.J. say, "Nice, Ms. W."

"What?" Surely Carter didn't message my student about our date last night. And my question is quickly answered, although I'm not sure how much I feel about the picture that E.J. flashes me from his phone. Taking the device, I look at the shot of me smiling at Carter from across the table at the steak house. *Cute.* But then I register the caption on the photo, and let the fact sink in that this is a published article that I had no control over. *Uh-oh.* "Number One Fan really is a fan of Carter Barlowe's after all. Looks like he's officially off the market."

He's news. I knew this. But it's supposed to be about his pitching. I even understood the stupid fan-at-the-game-who-brings-a-book coverage. But I hadn't expected a picture of our date would have my student trying to give me a congratulatory fist bump. "Sit down, Ernest. Now."

His demeanor changes at the realization that I don't share in his excitement. My dating life *will not* be a hot topic of conversation in this classroom.

I mindlessly go through the motions during the class period as the picture flashes through my mind several times. It had been a fabulous date. But I'd been naive to not consider who was sitting across the table from me.

The second period bell rings and Carter appears in the doorway, accepting a congratulatory fist bump from E.J. before moving into the classroom and, for the first time, shutting the door behind him.

"Joe called me. By that time, you were already in class. I tried to call, but your phone went to voice mail."

"It's too much."

"Avery, it'll be old news before lunchtime; someone else will be the topic of conversation."

"No, Carter, you're not hearing me. I can't do this. This is too much." I hold up my phone, the alerts steadily going off. "There are people contacting me that I haven't spoken to in years. People are sending me messages, asking random questions about our date."

"You didn't seem to mind the attention when it was focused on your parents' place of business." His accusatory tone only furthers my anger with the circus taking place around us.

"You did that with the feed store, not me. I never asked you to do anything." I point to the cup of coffee and reach into the desk, grabbing out the key fob for his truck. Handing it to him, I intone, "You need to leave."

"You're scared. But it's not of the attention or any of that bullshit. Something else keeps you wanting to run." Dropping the key fob on my desktop, he makes no move to leave.

"Get. Out."

He does an assessment, a slow scan of my face that feels more invasive than when he actually had his hands on me. "I'm scared too. Which is why I threw the signing event in your face, but I shouldn't have. That was my doing. And I did it for you. And I'm sorry, Avery. But I'm terrified I'm going to lose you before we've ever had a chance to give *us* a real shot."

His words hit more nerves than I care to admit because I want there to be an us, but I'm not sure if I can handle it.

Taking a deliberate step towards me. His voice is softer but still carries an accusatory tone that makes me feel like he can see straight through me. "What is it? What is it that you're scared of? You can't hide behind those romance books forever. And you're too smart to bury your head in the sand."

"You have no room to lecture me on hiding my head in the sand when you let everyone believe that Cash is some great baseball hero."

"You're right. But I know I'm a liar, and I know why I do it. I'm not running from the truth. I don't want to answer the questions that follow the truth because I'd have to relive every broken bone, bloodied nose, and blackened eye over and over in front of the entire world, and I chose to not fuckin' do it. But it's not out of fear, it's out of self-preservation. Because I want to murder the bastard every time I picture the moments he put his hands on my mother or she allowed him to hit me."

I take a step back, breaking away from his anger as I shake my head. "Carter."

He curses under his breath, moving to stand in front of me. There's still a rigidness in his posture, but his tone is low. "Avery, tell me what the hell to do to fix this, because you know damn well neither of us wants to walk away from this ... from us."

When I don't respond, he shifts closer, cautiously wrapping an arm around my lower back. Slowly, as if I'm the most fragile, delicate thing he's ever handled, he pulls me into a secure embrace that was made for me. He makes me feel safe and warm, like I should never be anywhere other than his arms ever again. Which will make it hurt all the worse when it's taken away for whatever reason.

"Tell me what you need. We can lay low, stay out of sight. I can ask for them to respect your privacy—although it's at their discretion to respect my wishes or not. I can get you a new phone number. I can answer your phone and tell each one of them to leave you alone. Ave, I know you're scared. I am too. But as much as this scares me, walking away from you scares me even more."

"I don't know how to do this."

"Me either, but we'll figure it out together." He bends down to place a kiss on my forehead. "I should've thought to warn you last night, but I was so damn thrilled you agreed to a date, I didn't think that far ahead."

"It's a lot to take in. Especially when my student *congratulates* me and keeps informing me of how many different websites my face is on."

"I'm sorry," he says, and I truly believe him. He's had to deal with this stuff his whole life, so he honestly knows how a few pictures have frazzled my nerves.

"Can I see you after the game tonight? We can order in and maybe *actually* watch a movie. Or just hang out. It's not even a school night."

"Okay. Let's hang out at my place."

"Sounds like a plan. Send me your address, and I'll pick up some supper on the way over."

I agree, moving away from him as he hesitantly steps back.

"We'll figure this out, Avery. We have to."

20

CARTER

"Looking good, Lowe," Coach Dundee says as I wrap up my workout in the bullpen. He's quiet a beat before coming to stand in front of me. "Are you ready for next week?"

I get what he's asking. He doesn't want to know if my arm will be ready, he wants to know if my mind is prepared as I'll be starting the first game of a four-game series on the road against my old team. The one that dropped me at the first sign of trouble with my arm. "Yeah. All good."

"Let me know if that changes."

"Aye aye, captain." I give him a smug look to mask my unease, and he shakes his head and walks away. Making my way to the clubhouse, I shower and get ready for tonight's game. I'll be supporting the team from the dugout, but it's my postgame plans that I'm really looking forward to.

"How's Avery?" Brooks asks as he steps next to me.

"Adjusting," I admit honestly.

"You are a lot to put up with," Brooks teases but he's not that far off.

"Yeah. Aren't we all." I nod at Gunner bouncing around the clubhouse, completely naked. He whoops and hollers, trying to get everyone fired up. Most everyone looks at him like he's insane, but that doesn't slow his roll.

After the game, I can't get to Avery's place fast enough. She said she wasn't hungry, which is understandable considering the time of night it is, so it's fine by me—no stops necessary between the field and my girl. But I'm not completely happy until the moment she opens the door of her apartment. Those hazel eyes hit me, and I take in her casual appearance. Her fingers pick at the hem of her tank top, pulling it down slightly as she invites me in. She rubs her hands over her cotton pajama pants, and even though she looks uncertain, she doesn't look uncomfortable. Good enough for me. And I don't blame her for being more at ease as I look around the small but cozy living area that connects to the kitchen, a bar separating the two. I drop my key fob and phone on the counter as soon as I'm within reach. I resist mauling her, but just barely. Instead, I pull her against me and savor her mouth on mine, her body pressed firmly against my torso until she slightly leans back. "Hi."

"Hi," I smile. "I've been waiting to do that for a while." I stamp a quick kiss on her mouth before releasing her. She stands still, watching me in a daze for a few seconds before we take a seat on her couch.

She's right, her place would fit in my oversized kitchen. Yet, I'd pick this place any day over mine. And I don't believe I feel that way only because it's hers. There's something homey about it. But then again, that *could* be only because of her.

"What do you want to watch?" She flips through a few movies, but I remain silent. I could watch her all night if it were up to me. I love seeing her so much more relaxed than she'd been last night, and especially this morning, at my place. It's only been seconds, but I already want her mouth back on mine.

When I don't respond, she looks to me with a soft smile. Leaning closer, I bring my lips to hers, patiently savoring, tasting her as my hand grips the nape of her neck. Every ounce of me wants to feel her, have every bit of her right this second but I know I have to be patient with her, and I will because I want more than a one and done.

As she leans into me, I tell myself to slow down, but it doesn't stop me from guiding her onto my lap to straddle me. Her kisses become more eager, but something still tells me she isn't ready to completely surrender her body to me. Maybe just a little taste will help because I'm about to go out of my mind. My hands slip into the waistband of her pajama pants, smoothing over her skin as I look to her. "I want to touch you."

The light in her eyes burns more intense as she returns her mouth to mine. I take it as my cue to proceed, especially when her fingers grip the material of my T-shirt as her ass rubs against me.

Sliding my hands into her panties, I grip her ass, pulling her down as I shift up, letting her feel what she's doing to me because I'm pretty sure I'm about to bust out of my damn jeans. The soft gasp that escapes her lips thrills me as much as touching her because I know she's enjoying this too. Maneuvering my hand around her hip, I skim her soft skin with my fingertips as I move between her thighs. Cupping her against my palm, I rub my thumb in just the right spot, and she responds by shifting into it. Slipping my fingers inside her, I follow her lead as she rides my hand. Her eyes close as her head falls back, pure pleasure on her face. Holy shit. She looks so sexy. I'm convinced she could get me off without ever touching me, especially if we stay like we are.

Her sex clenches around my fingers, and her nails dig into my shoulders as she stills. I watch her ride out her release, the pleasure plain on her face, but she has no idea how much I'm getting out of this as well. Will she ever know what she does to me? I don't understand it yet, so I doubt she ever will.

When her eyes open and look to me, there's a bit of blush on her cheeks. Removing my fingers from her, I grip her hips and give her a lazy, savoring kiss. "That was so fucking hot, Avery."

The blush deepens on her cheeks, and I fully expect her to shy away. She doesn't. And it sends an even greater thrill throughout me when she keeps her mouth on mine, her fingers reaching between us to unbutton my jeans.

"You don't have to. I mean, I want you to. But you don't have to." I'd be happy with just the memory of having my hands on her.

"I want to." Her words fill my ears as she pushes my boxers down, freeing me. As she takes me in her hand and strokes me, a sexy smile breaks out across her face.

I laugh at myself internally because I know I'm not gonna last long. I can't remember the last time I had a hand job, and though it should sound juvenile, with Avery's hand on me, it's the hottest damn thing. Shit, it's been too long, and I'd like to use that as an excuse but that's not it. It's her. It's Avery that's bringing me such pleasure.

She maintains a perfect grip, moving up and down, stroking the length of me in a sublime rhythm. Her sweet mouth remains on mine. Reaching up, I slide my fingers into her hair, slightly gripping as I keep her lips on mine. Kissing, teasing, savoring every second of her touch on me until my body stiffens, my hand quickly reaching between us as I spill into it.

"Fuck. That was hot too." I give her smiling lips another

smooch, feeling like a hormonal teenager as she moves off my lap. Quickly slipping into the bathroom, I clean up and head back out to the living room. For a second, I literally hold my breath, worried she's going to regret what just happen.

When she glances over her shoulder from where she's comfortably seated on the couch, her lips stretch into a gorgeous smile that allows me to exhale any and all worry as she asks, "So what movie do you want to watch?"

"Anything is good." And damn it, it is. I could watch grass grow and be happy as long as she's snuggled up next to me. And that's what she does as I take a seat next to her.

"Be careful with that answer. That response once scored Bodie an all-day marathon of *Harry Potter.*" Her smile is directed at me, but I can't help but feel a bit jealous at their connection.

"Sign me up."

She continues clicking through until she selects a movie. "Sorry it's such a boring Friday night."

"I can't think of anywhere else I'd rather be." I smile as she looks up to me. "Seriously. I don't need anything but your company to enjoy my Friday night."

"Good one." She playfully teases as she focuses back on the TV. "Bodie complains because I'd rather stay in."

"Eh. Going out is overrated. It never aligned with my goals, so I never felt the need to indulge. Zero FOMO for me." I hesitate for a second before asking, "Did y'all ever date?"

She chuckles, shaking her head. "Never. He's like the brother I wished I had instead of Rhett. I can't live without him. Even Mom says he's her long-lost son and requires his attendance at Sunday family lunches. She lets him have it every time he misses."

Why does that not ease my jealousy? Not one damn bit.

I'm not normally an envious person—but maybe I've never had anyone in my life worth getting possessive over.

"Your mom invited me to join y'all." And the invitation made me way too happy. "But I explained with the game schedule it isn't doable."

"Yes, I'm sure she understands."

"She did. She's a sweet lady. I assured her I'd attend during off-season though."

Her eyes dart to me.

"What?"

"Nothing. Just surprised you're planning so far ahead."

Me too. "Well, from the sound of it, her cooking is the best around."

"Truth." She relaxes against me as she talks with such affection about her mom, and I honestly enjoy watching her more than the movie. Eventually, she's sound asleep in my arms, and it's unnerving how far ahead into the future I can envision being with this woman. Because I've only ever wanted one thing long term. Could only fathom loving one thing enough to plan my life around.

Suddenly, there's a second competing with the first, and I haven't the foggiest idea how to reconcile that. There's no film to review with Dundee, no stats to study and memorize in order to devise a game plan to follow. There's only my heart to guide me, and it's without a doubt the only muscle I've ignored and disregarded in all my years of training.

21

AVERY

"He's coming over again?" Bodie says on the other end of the line. "Well, I guess you don't have time for us peons anymore."

There's a joking tone in his voice, but I don't think he's fully teasing. "You can still come over."

"Nah, I have some work to catch up on, anyway. I guess I'll just see my infamous best friend at her mom's house tomorrow for family lunch. Unless you're too busy for that too."

"Shut up. You're the one who told me to give Carter a chance, so you can't be salty about it now."

"I'm not, Avery. I'm happy for you. Just be careful. I don't want to see you get hurt again."

"Wow. The vote of confidence is reassuring."

"You know what I mean. He's still a jock under all that rescue-the-family-business persona."

"The business wasn't in trouble, so it wasn't technically a rescue." Even if it has increased business a ton.

"Okay. Well, I'll see you at your parents' tomorrow."

"Are you not picking me up?" He always does, it's usually

a given whenever he attends. We ride together since my place is on his way.

"Yeah. No prob. Wasn't sure if Carter was driving you."

"He has a game, but you already knew that."

His laugh doesn't make me feel any better because I don't understand his issue. "Well, maybe put in a word for me sometime. A star on the podcast could really set us apart."

And there it is. "I'll ask." *That won't be awkward*, but I'll try for Bodie.

After disconnecting the call, I turn off the game that I shouldn't be watching anyway and decide to read for a while instead. As always, I get lost in the book, the time totally getting away from me. It's late when I glance up at the clock, so I put the book aside and tidy up my apartment for a little while, then shower and put on a movie. Eventually, there's a knock on the door.

Like the teenagers I teach, a giddy, excited feeling swirls in my gut as I open the door to find Carter smiling back at me. He leans over, plants a lingering kiss on me, then moves past me into my place.

"I didn't think the game was ever going to end." He drops his phone and keys in the same spot as last night.

"*I know.* Nineteen innings are way too many to sit through," I tease as he grins.

"For sure." He pulls me to him, kissing me thoroughly before leaning back. "Gunner said to tell you hi and that he's glad you've finally given my sorry ass a chance because I'm more fun to be around now."

"Gunner?" The name sounds familiar, but I can't quite place it.

"You really don't follow the team." His smile reaches his eyes. "Gunner is the shortstop and always the loudest one in the room. One of the most well-known players around here too."

"I've only watched a few games, but I thought I recognized the name." They're all new to me, but I do recall the broadcaster talking about him now.

"I have to tell him that you didn't know who he is. Hopefully it'll knock Gunner down a few notches because he's still giving me shit about you reading during my Coyote debut."

"Yeah. Sorry not sorry." I sit on the couch and Carter joins me, the movie still playing.

"Eh. It's all in good fun. The guys really have given me a warmer welcome than I imagined."

"Bodie said you're starting next week against your old team."

He gives me a puzzled look before nodding. "Yep. It's not something I'm looking forward to. But it is what it is. Their decision to cut me after my injury was a business decision, so I get it." He lets out an exaggerated breath before finishing. "It was more the uncertainty of not knowing for sure if I'd play again that sent me reeling. Until the Coyotes called." He chuckles, "Out of all the teams, it was them. At the time, I thought it was the worst thing ever. Now, I realize I was one lucky bastard to be brought back here."

I don't want to read between the lines, but I secretly thank whoever within the organization decided bringing Carter here was a good idea. For his sake and mine.

We settle into what is becoming our comfy position on the couch together as I half-watch the movie. There won't be an ideal time, so I just go for it. "Bodie wanted me to ask you something. You can say no, though. Of course, you can always say no."

He reaches up, rubbing his thumb over my lips as he halts my rambling. "Just ask."

"He wanted to see if you'd be a guest on the podcast he does with his brothers. It's all about baseball and it was the reason he wanted to go to the game that day. Something to do with atmosphere or something."

"Yes." His word halts my second rambling session as I look to him.

"You don't have to."

"I know. I want to. He's important to you. And it's the least I can do after he talked you into attending that game."

"Yeah. Apparently, it was like a big deal or something." I roll my eyes, attempting to brush off how much him doing this for Bodie means to me.

"Best game ever. For more than one reason." His meaning is clear as he shifts forward, pressing his lips to mine. The kiss starts out soft, patient, but soon becomes intense as I let him guide me back, and we settle against the seat of the sofa. Like it's the most natural thing in the world, he moves his body over mine. As his hand runs up my thigh, his mouth drops to my neck, his lips vibrating against my skin. "Tell me to stop, Avery."

"I don't want you to stop," I admit. Why this truth frightens me, I'm not sure, but damn, I might cry if he stops. *He cannot stop.* Not an option.

Spurred on by my response, he presses against me, allowing me to feel exactly how much he's enjoying this, and it only drives my desire to have more of him. His mouth is everywhere, feverishly devouring my lips, tasting my neck, nipping at my earlobe. When he leans slightly back, we're of the same mind. Together, we both grip the hem of his T-shirt, lifting it up and over his head before he slings it to the floor. There's a hungry, determined need in his eyes that lights me up inside. I want nothing more than for him to fulfil whatever it is he's thinking.

His hand moves under my shirt, and I arch off the couch to allow for him to push the fabric up over my head before tossing it aside to join his on the floor. Carter's sultry lips travel to my chest, exploring thoroughly as he reaches behind my back. His skillful fingers expertly unclasp my bra in what could be the swiftest, smoothest removal ever. I feel the fabric give way and fall from my chest, immediately replaced by his mouth. His tongue teases my nipple as I lift to him. Damn, is this how it's really supposed to feel? Because no one has *ever* touched me like this or made me feel so much. Carter pulls at my desire and makes me crave more. I want his hands and mouth on me everywhere. All at once. The passion he's ignited is intense.

His fingers move down, hooking into the waistband of my yoga pants. Dragging the fabric down my legs, he pulls them off along with my panties in one fluid movement before returning his mouth to my skin. He licks, nips, and sucks, playful and reverential at the same time. His tongue trails along my stomach as he slowly moves down, positioning his shoulders between my thighs. His mouth covers me as his hand grips the inside of my knee, pushing my leg open until it's resting on the couch's seat. Having gained more access, his tongue circles my sex, and I rock against his mouth, half out of my mind already. A sultry laugh vibrates against me, teasing me for only a moment because in the next, there's no laughter. Only gasps, moans, and heaving breaths as Carter pulls every bit of pleasure out of me.

I ride the wave for longer than I knew was possible, and all too soon, his tongue charts a course back up my body. Skimming over my torso, licking each breast, tasting the column of my neck, he doesn't stop his ascent until his mouth is back on mine. Even though he's already surrounding me, pulling at me in every good way possible, I want to feel more. Reaching down, I unbutton his jeans and slide under the denim and his boxer briefs to take him in my hand. I only stroke him once, and he tenses under my touch.

Cursing softly under his breath, he returns his lips to

mine. Planting a foot on the floor, he wraps both arms around my back, hugging my torso to his as he stands, bringing me with him. He's so strong and the change of position happened so quickly, the momentum makes wrapping my legs around his waist an easy task, especially when his hands grip my ass. We kiss the entire way as he carries me to the bedroom, our chests smashed together, my fingers tangling in his dark-brown hair.

Moving to the side of the bed, he kicks off his jeans after lowering me to the mattress. He grabs a condom and rolls it on while kneeling on the mattress. Then he moves me back and hovers over me, reaching between us before his nude body moves against mine. His feverish kiss slows, then he looks down and asks, "Are you sure, Avery?"

"Yes," I say, part gasp, part desperate plea.

His mouth quickly drops back to cover mine as his hand grips my thigh, hooking it over his hip. He remains still for a few seconds, and anticipation surges through my veins. Breaking our kiss, his hooded eyes linger on my mouth for a second, then zip up to meet my eyes the moment he pushes inside me. My jaw drops open in a silent gasp of rapture, and his eyes dart back down to my mouth.

He remains still for a second before nearly pulling out of me, then rocks back inside on a groan. I match his rhythm as I rise to take him again and again, eagerly receiving each thrust. Carter fills me perfectly, it's like we were made for each other. It's not my first time, but it might as well be, because no man has ever made me feel anything close to what Carter does.

Wrapping my arms around his neck, I cling to him as his pace picks up before he goes still. An exaggerated groan that's part nonsensical words and part my name rumbles quietly out of him, telling me that I've made him feel the same way he's made me. Or at least I hope so, because the only thing I can think right now is that I want to do this again (and again and again), but only with him.

He remains inside me, propped up on his elbow to lazily kiss me, savoring the moment before gradually pulling out. "I'll be right back," he says, moving to the bathroom.

Once he's taken care of business and has come out, I quickly trade places with him, shutting the door and taking a second to consider what's happened between us. I have no regrets about it, and hopefully it stays that way. After cleaning up, I return to find him sitting back against my headboard, still in all his nude glory. There's no choice but for me to take in his muscular frame. Damn. I had no idea what was under that shirt, but I'm glad I got to find out. His sexy grin tells me he doesn't mind me checking him out. And in fact, he stands, moving in front of me. His arms encircle me, his hands caressing up my back then down, gripping my backside as he leans to whisper in my ear.

"Hope you like what you see." He knows he's hot as hell, but his playful arrogance shines through, a perfect combo for post-sex flirting. "Because I'll never get enough of you."

Ditto. But I keep that thought to myself as we shuffle-kiss our way back to the bed and slide under the covers. As Carter spoons me, his arm wrapped snuggly around my middle while dropping kisses on my shoulder, the only thing that feels out of place is how right and natural it feels. I drift off to sleep wrapped in the security of his embrace and a strangely contented peace.

22

CARTER

This is one of the few mornings since falling in love with baseball that I can recall not wanting to get out of bed and head to the field. Of course, I haven't ever had Avery's nude body draped across me, either. Smoothing my hand up her back, she snuggles closer to me then gradually comes to consciousness and realizes I'm in her bed. She looks at me with a bit of shock and fantastically hot bed head.

"Good morning." I clear my throat when my unused voice comes out gravelly and rough. She returns the greeting and slides out of bed, heading straight to the bathroom. There's no point in her freaking out because she's not going anywhere, not after last night for sure. I only thought I was engrossed in her before. Now that I've *really* experienced her, felt what it'd be like to wake up next to her every morning, there's no way I could ever let her go.

Getting out the bed, I pull on my black boxer briefs and impatiently wait for her to exit the bathroom. When she does, she avoids making eye contact with me as she slips into a T-shirt and pair of pajama pants, then heads wordlessly out of the bedroom, so I follow. Avery Whitlock is not going to run from me again. She can't. She wants this as much as I do, I just need her to not get spooked and dart for the hills. Once in the kitchen, she fills the coffee maker's carafe with water and proceeds to busy herself with making a pot.

"Avery, are we okay?"

Her body tenses for a moment before she eases. "Yep. Just making you some coffee for a change."

The playfulness in her voice says more than her words to my relief. Stepping in front of her, I wrap my arms around her. "I bet it'll be the best coffee ever."

A knock sounds on the door, and I lose her soft skin under my hands as she wiggles out of my arms. But the ease that finally appeared in her posture is what I'd wanted to hold onto a little bit longer.

She looks out the peephole before glancing back to me, her eyes dropping to my bare chest, but then she swings the door open.

"Morning," Bodie's chipper voice greets her. That happy attitude changes real quick when his eyes land on me. "I see you didn't take my advice."

"What advice?" I ask by way of greeting, tipping my chin up to him in what I'm trying to keep as a casual *Hey, what's up, man?* acknowledgment. Really wanting to know what advice he gave his best friend, I have a sinking feeling it's not favorable for me. *Damn it, Bodie.* I'm having a hell of a time fighting to keep her from running away from me as is without him putting even more shit in her head. She said they're only friends. Is that his choice or hers?

Avery pulls him into the apartment and shuts the door. "You're early."

"Obviously." He doesn't look my way. "Your dad wanted me to help him with the shelving rebuild before lunch."

The game is even less appealing now, knowing I'll be

missing Whitlock family lunch while Bodie is there with Avery, Lyle, and the entire bunch.

"Give me a few minutes to get dressed." She moves into the kitchen, grabs out a coffee mug, and fills it. Passing it to me, she repeats the process for herself. "Oh, Carter agreed to do the podcast interview."

Bodie watches me as he says, "I'm sure Carter agreed to a lot last night."

"Bodie," Avery scolds him, slamming her cup on the counter.

I can't blame the guy. I'd be terrified of losing her too. Although, he might as well get used to it because I'm not going anywhere. I slip a hand onto her hip, giving Bodie an unbothered, friendly expression, especially after she leans into me. "It's the least I can do for you bringing her to my game."

His face tightens as he lets out a laugh. "Yeah, she wasn't happy to see *Baby Cash* play, for sure. Her nickname, not mine."

Fuck. That one stings.

On a sharp inhalation of breath, Avery whips her head to look at me. "That was before— I didn't even know you. He'd told me how much he wanted to see the game because you were starting." She turns a frustrated look to her best friend.

Bodie doesn't pay her any mind. "Speaking of, don't you have one to get to now?"

"Yep. I should get going since I've missed warm-ups."

His condescending, big brother attitude kicks into full gear as he asks with a sarcastic chuckle, "Was that really a wise choice with the big return to your home turf tomorrow?"

Probably not. "I'm more than ready." At least I should be. Only, I wish Avery was going with me. "I really should get going though." Once I'm in the bedroom, I hear quiet bickering between them.

Bodie didn't seem to have any issue with me before, but I really hope it's only his protective-friend instinct flaring up and that he'll simmer down once Avery sets him straight. Because if he's feeling some kind of way, a lifelong friendship will be hard to compete with if he decides to make a move.

The room goes silent when I step back in. But I still see the look she's giving him, a nonverbal *Chill out*, reminding me of siblings who have a language all their own. That both makes me happy for the two of them, and jealous once again at the connection I'll never have a chance of competing with. With my jeans on, I grab my T-shirt from the living room floor before moving to her. For a second, I fear she'll pull away, but she doesn't, instead wrapping her arms around my neck as she kisses me back. Bodie and Avery might have a brother-sister language, but there's no way they have the gut-level passion between them that her and I do, reiterated by the way her hands move to my chest, her fingers gripping my T-shirt like she can't hold on tight enough. And I know that feeling.

A loud, obvious throat clearing sounds. And while I want him to know she's mine and I intend on sticking around, I don't want to damage the friendship I hope I can have with her best friend. He's important to her. So, he's important to me. As I shift away, her grip tightens, her lips lingering for a few more seconds before she releases me. Yep. We're more than okay.

"Here." She passes me a travel mug. "So you don't fall asleep at the field. It really puts some people's jock straps in a twist when that happens."

Shit. Her gorgeous smile reaches her eyes and takes ahold of any remaining sliver within me that wasn't already hers.

All I can do in response is place another quick kiss on her smiling lips.

I hold up the pink cup, donning yellow and blue llamas as I hear Bodie snicker. "Oh, it's serious now. That's her favorite one. She won't let me take it without a lecture to not lose it."

"Yep, 'cause you lose everything or forget to bring it back." She gives him an annoyed look before turning to me. "It is my favorite though."

"I'm sure the guys will love it." I know I do even if it's something as silly as a cup because that means she plans on keeping me around. "I'll call you later."

With that, I give her a lingering kiss, painfully pulling away before I walk out. My coffee-filled llama cup in hand, I'm unable to remove the goofy grin from my face.

23

AVERY

"What the hell was that about?" I ask Bodie as Carter shuts the door behind him.

"Nothing." He casually shrugs, walks to the kitchen, and pours himself a cup of coffee. Like he's done a million times. But this time is different. There's a loaded silence, and I'm not so convinced it's "nothing" as I stand, waiting for an explanation.

"I told you to be careful, then I find him naked in your damn kitchen."

"You also told me to give him a chance. Or did you say that because you never thought he'd actually be interested in me?"

"Avery, really? I don't want to see you get used. Why else would Carter agree to do a podcast that has a whole twenty listeners, including my mom?"

"Maybe because he's a nice guy."

"Sure." His bitter laugh makes me feel like he thinks I'm a fool for actually believing Carter could be a good guy. What he doesn't know is Carter has shown me a side of him he hasn't shown anyone. But I'd never dare say that. Because unlike Bodie, Carter trusts me and my judgment. At least, that's what it feels like right now.

"You go ahead. I'll take my truck when I'm ready to go."

"Avery, don't be ridiculous."

"I'm not trying to." I take in a deep breath, exhaling as I look to the guy I've called my best friend my entire life. "I'm having a hard enough time adjusting to whatever this is going on between me and Carter, the last thing I need is my best friend insinuating I'm a fool."

"You're not a fool, Avery. He would be if he couldn't see how great you are. And maybe I'm a little worried about him hurting you because it's my fault for dragging you to the game in the first place. And maybe … I'm afraid of losing my best friend to Carter Barlowe." He takes in a breath and says, "Go get dressed. I'll drive us to your parents' place, and you can tell me how wonderful Baby Cash is."

"Don't call him that." My response is a little quick as Bodie gives me a confused look. "Just call him Carter. You know, like he's a regular guy who I'd like to get to know better?"

"Sure. Hurry up, so we can get done with the shelving and watch your *regular guy* on TV."

"Whatever," I mumble heading to my room to get dressed. Yes, Carter Barlowe is on TV today, but he's just Carter when he's with me.

24

CARTER

Sure enough. The guys didn't disappoint. Six hours later, they're still giving me shit about arriving to the field with my colorful travel mug this morning. Even as we prepare to leave for the airport, they're not letting it die. And I don't care one damn bit.

Road games have never bothered me in the past, but right now, I don't want to get on the plane. It's not our awaiting opponents—although I should be focused on them, especially after the ass-chewing Dundee gave me for missing warm-ups this morning.

And he's right, my head isn't in the game. But I don't think it's solely because of Avery. She's just the perfect distraction to avoid what I know is inevitable. Cash Barlowe.

Reaching for my phone, I type out exactly what I'm thinking.

Me: I want you to go with me.

Avery: I can't. I have work.

Me: I know. But that doesn't stop me from wanting you with me.

A week. I'll be away from her light for a damn week. Why does that seem too long all of a sudden?

Coach Dundee gives me a judgy look before stepping in front of me. "Ready to go?"

"Yeah." I respond as he turns to walk away. He won't like the question, and it's not his job to train me outside of the game, but I ask him anyway. "How do you get used to leaving?"

"You don't," he responds, dropping to sit next to me. "But the wife and kids know it's part of the job."

"A part that I never gave much thought to until I had someone to leave behind."

He gives a knowing nod. News of Avery and me hasn't exactly been kept quiet around the clubhouse, so Dundee knows damn well what I'm talking about.

With an encouraging pat on the shoulder, he says, "But that someone who makes leaving hard, makes coming home even better. So, get your head in the game, Lowe."

"Will do."

Eventually.

Hopefully.

Me: Plan on watching the game tomorrow?

Avery: Yes.

Me: Reading-watching or watching-watching?

Avery: The latter. Probably.

A smile stretches across my face. It helps get my head in the game knowing she'll be watching.

Grabbing my bag, I head out to board the bus that will take us to the airport. Even if my head is in the game, I already can't wait to step off this bus next week, knowing she'll be waiting for me.

25

AVERY

There's no chance any book could pull my attention away from watching Carter on TV right now.

"Your *regular guy* is looking pretty nervous right now."

I slap Bodie's shoulder but keep my eyes glued on Carter. Ugh—he's right though. There's hesitation in Carter that I haven't seen from him before. I squint, watching as he removes his hat and looks at something inside. He uses the sleeve of his jersey to wipe his brow before putting his hat back on, then settles into his stance before the windup.

"What's in his hat?" I wonder aloud.

"Cheat sheet kind of, but totally allowed," Bodie responds as Carter sends another pitch directly over the plate, untouched. Bodie clenches his fist in unison with the umpire's gesture, calling the strike. Seconds later, Carter's old teammate is out of the batter's box, walking away from the plate back to the dugout. "Another inning down."

We sit and watch the remainder of the game, my attention fully focused until Carter's last out in the sixth inning. When the Coyotes take the field in the seventh, another guy is on the mound, so my investment in the game wanes. The Coyotes take home the win, and I know that has to be a good feeling for him. It must be satisfying to go there and prove what he needed to himself more so than anyone else.

"Your boy delivered." Bodie slaps my leg, rising from the couch before stretching. "I'm gonna head home. Early morning."

"Same." Never could have predicted I'd be up late watching a baseball game of all things on a school night.

"You know, if anything, I'm grateful Carter has you watching the games without complaint."

"I'll remember that next time." And I'll be sure to find something to complain about just because.

Lying in my empty bed, I'm having a hard time falling asleep when my phone lights up with a message I'm way too happy to see.

Carter: So was it a watching-watching night?

Me: Yes. The first two-thirds of the game definitely captured my attention.

Carter: Awesome. Are you gonna be up for a while?

I shouldn't be.

Me: Probably so. Can't sleep.

Instead of a message, my phone rings as I see Carter's contact flash across the screen. When I answer, he says, "I can't sleep either."

Tomorrow will be a long day, but I settle in, wanting to stay on the phone as long as possible. The conversation flows naturally until I say, "Yeah, but my students don't get a cheat sheet for their tests."

"I don't have a cheat sheet."

"But I saw you looking in your hat, and Bodie said that's what y'all have in your hats."

"It is for most guys, but I don't need a cheat sheet though.

Memorizing the lineup is always something I study beforehand."

"Then what were you looking at?"

"I've never showed it to anyone. Not even my pitching coach knows what I keep in my hat. He knows it's not a cheat sheet, but it's what I've always needed to keep me focused."

"You don't have to tell me."

He lets out a soft laugh. "I want to show you."

My phone dings with a message, and I see a text from Carter containing a picture. Putting him on speaker, I open the message, and the enlarged photo comes into view. It's a baseball card. A Coyote one of a young Cash Barlowe that's laminated and worn at the edges. In the features of the young player, I see similarities to Carter, but what my eyes focus on is the writing across the card—the same words I've heard him say. *For me, not him.*

"I needed my career to be mine, not something I did out of spite, even if it started out that way. He took so much from me; I wouldn't allow him to take a game that I love and turn it into something I hated as much as I hate him. Because he tried."

"I don't know how you do it. Pretend like everything is okay when it's not."

"I had plenty of practice growing up." He pauses for a second before saying, "But some days are harder than others."

He quickly changes the subject, lightening the topic as he asks about Finn, and I follow his lead. But the picture of young Cash Barlowe stays in my mind. It's not the retired baseball legend who consumes my mind though. It's his son who's put on a show, keeping the horror of growing up with the monster locked inside. Especially after hearing some of what occurred during his childhood, my heart aches for the ten-year-old with his arm in a cast who still covers the pain with a smile, but I'm thankful he trusts me enough to confide in me. Carter doesn't appear on the surface to be struggling, but something tells me he's still working to escape the ghost of a man who lingers in the shadows. How could he not?

26

CARTER

The week on the road has had plenty ups and downs, but the highlight of each day was always when I talked to Avery about everything and nothing. There's no comparison to being with her, though, and I'm trying to be patient. Damn, it's difficult.

Because I can't slow my roll where she's concerned, I'd asked her before the game this morning if I could stop by on my way home from the stadium after we traveled back. So when I pull up to her apartment, I opt to leave my bag in my truck. Planning to play it cool, I figure if everything goes well, I can avoid going to my house altogether and simply "remember" I have my bag out in my truck. Lame, but I want her to want me to stay. I shouldn't just assume she's okay with it after being away from her for the week.

The door of her apartment flies open, and the gorgeous sight of her smile and sparkling eyes send all thoughts of anything but her right out the window. Stepping inside, I wrap an arm around her, bringing her lips to mine. I walk her back until she's pressed up against the wall, then I pull her slightly forward, grip her ass, and lift. Her legs wrap around my waist as I lean into her.

Her arms snake around my neck and I'm unable to suppress my smile. "I've been wanting to do that the entire damn week." Coach was right. Leaving her had been difficult but coming home to her is hot as hell.

"Me too," she laughs, leaning in to kiss me again. When my phone rings, she pulls back, watching me. "You gonna get that?"

"Nope."

"Carter ..." She attempts to squirm out of my arms.

"Avery," I say with mock seriousness, to which she stills, eyebrows shooting up in question, "my hands are on your ass. They'll leave a message if it's important."

She smiles and rolls her eyes, but she likes it as much as I do. "You should answer it. It's late, so I'm sure they're calling for a reason."

I don't want to let her go, but she's adamant, so I officially trash my playing-it-cool plan. "Am I staying here tonight?"

Her eyes don't meet mine as she says, "I hope so."

"Remember where we left off." The promise of a night in her bed is enough for me to release her temporarily but not before I give her another quick kiss, then I set her back on her feet.

Pulling the phone out of my pocket, I see Dundee's number. This better be good. "Yes, Coach?" I ask, watching as Avery walks into her kitchen, grabs a bottle of water, and props her hip against the counter. I follow her, accepting the bottle she offers me as Dundee continues his lecture from the plane. I had one rough inning yesterday, and he's been on my ass nonstop. I've reassured him it was a fluke—I messed up, made a few wrong calls, and paid the price by giving up two RBIs and then a home run.

"Lowe, it's important that we stay on track. All season. You'll be there tomorrow for warm-ups, right?"

"Yes, sir. I'll be there."

"I'll believe it when I see it. Although, even seeing your decision to change from a splitter to a four-seamer for Hastings was unbelievable. We went over the lineup, and I know you knew the best call." Dundee's frustration matches my own, but mine is a little less on the surface than his. I know I made the wrong call which was shaking off the first sign for a splitter from Lynch. Even he hesitated, giving me the splitter signal again before he moved to the next sign for a four-seam fastball.

"Yes. I get it. I shouldn't have shaken off the calls."

"Carter, a few bad calls can be the beginning of many."

Damn. One off inning and he's ready to yank me from the roster. Or, at least that's how it feels. "Then I'll be sure to not make any more bad calls. Like I told you during your trip to the mound in the fourth, I just needed to regroup, and I appreciated the blow. Then I proved it after you were back to the dugout, right?"

I hear a sputtering cough and look over to see Avery wiping her mouth, slapping her hand against her chest as she gives me a strange look. "Are you okay?" I ask her, and she quickly nods.

I figure the only thing I can do is show Coach I'm still in the game. I can have Avery and still be a good ball player. I can. Only right now, all I want to focus on is her after being deprived for a week. Plus, I'm still trying to figure out what's going on as she coughs again.

Needing to wrap up, I tell Dundee, "I'll be there early so we can review everything I did wrong once more."

"See you then, smart-ass." Coach finally hangs up and my full attention is on Avery and those reddened cheeks.

"Are you sure you're okay over there?"

"Yeah." She takes a sip of water, clearing her throat.

"What has you all choked up then?"

Her cheeks blush a bit more as she asks, "What exactly did you mean by your coach gave you a blow? Because you don't even want to know how I interpreted that."

"Well, well, well. Look which one of us has their mind in the gutter."

"Who wouldn't?" She throws her hands in the air. "You just said he gave you a blow, any normal person would draw the same conclusion."

"No, only a person who keeps her nose in those sexy books would interpret it like that." I enjoy seeing her frazzled at the thought of her mind in the gutter, because I know mine has been there more times than not when I think of her. "But in my world, blow means breather. He saw my head wasn't on straight, so he came out to the mound to settle me down. Gave me a few seconds to breathe."

She shakes her head. "Why don't y'all just say 'breather' when you mean 'breather'?" I shrug and throw her a face. "Still doesn't make sense to me, but okay. Glad your coach gave you a good blow and got you through the inning." She's unable to contain her laughter, and though it's at my expense, it's music to my ears.

Walking over to her, she smiles up at me when I stop in front of her. Placing a hand on the counter on either side of her, I kiss her smiling lips. "I missed you."

Her body tenses up a bit, then she relaxes against me, allowing me full access to savor her for a few seconds before she shifts back and says something else that is music to my ears. "I missed you too."

27

AVERY

It's too good to be true. It has to be.

We've fallen into an easy routine without any effort. He brings me coffee on my free period, heads off to the field, then crashes at my place after the game. Only now, our routine will be disturbed because he's leaving for another road trip next week. And I don't like how much I missed him last time—*before* we started spending every night together. This time is bound to be way worse since we've been together every moment that didn't involve my work or his time at the field.

"Summer vacay is coming up. Then you won't have an excuse not to travel with me," he suggests.

"Don't they have rules about that or something? I don't want to interfere with the game or Coach giving you a blow."

He laughs. "I like your blows better."

Okay. I opened the door and stepped right into that one. "We're in my *classroom*, Carter."

"Hey, you brought it up."

"Touché." I shake my head. "But really, you're busy with the games, and I don't want to be a distraction and take away from your team bonding. Plus, I usually work at the store during the summer. It's the busy season for my parents."

"Maybe just one road trip?"

"Coach won't like that." I know he's been riding Carter about keeping focused, and I don't want to be the one to disrupt him.

"Coach won't be in my room after the game, but I really would like you to be."

"Maybe," I say just to move on from the topic.

"I haven't heard much from E.J. lately. Everything good with him?" Carter asks.

"Yep. He's definitely been in full E.J. mode."

"That's good." I look to Carter, grateful that he cares enough to ask about one of my students. "What?"

"Nothing." I focus back on my phone, pushing away the premature thought. It's much too soon and ridiculously audacious. I wouldn't dare admit to him that I wonder what kind of father he would be. He didn't have a good example, that's for certain, but I can't see him being anything other than a great dad. At any rate, that's not something that should be anywhere in my psyche.

"I need to get going." He stands, placing the chair he'd been using back in its rightful spot before bending down to give me a kiss like it's the most natural gesture in the world. "I'll see you at home tonight."

Home.

"Actually, I promised Tessa that I'd watch Finn tonight."

"Oh, well I can swing by and hang with you and Finn after the game."

"He'll be asleep. Little kid, early bedtime."

"Okay. I guess I'll see you tomorrow, then."

"Actually, I'll be at the store this weekend. There's a big county fair that'll bring in extra customers."

The look on his face confirms he's seeing right through

my excuses. "If you need a little space, let me know. But please don't lie to me."

"I figured you'd be busy getting ready for the road trip and all. You haven't stayed at your house all week." I try to play off the comment, but I wonder if he really wants to be at my place or is catering to me because he knows I'm not comfortable at his.

"Yet, this town has felt more like home in the past week than it ever did growing up." He bends down, placing a tender kiss on my cheek before stepping back. "Call me if you have time."

Even after he disappears, I watch the doorway. Why do I feel like I just took three steps back? I spooked myself, sure. But I would have freaked him out too if he knew how much I didn't want to be away from him.

The rest of my day already feels off knowing he won't be part of the routine. That isn't necessarily a good thing or healthy mindset. No doubt he would hightail it out of here if he knew how much him calling my place *home* meant to me after I was imagining what type of father he would be. Oh, the places my mind can go so easily with him. Places that it shouldn't because I'm not who he wants me to be. I can't follow him around all summer with hopes of capturing a few minutes here and there.

I have my own life. If I make it all about him, it'll be harder to get back on track when he leaves. And he will, he said it. Canaan Falls long term isn't his plan, not with Cash here, and I can't imagine living anywhere else. I'm right back where I started weeks ago: Nothing about Carter Barlowe and me make sense.

28

CARTER

I know I have too much damn time on my hands. Why else would I be sitting in the driveway of my mom's house on a Sunday evening? Maybe it's the fact that my phone hasn't rang or received one message from Avery since I walked out of her classroom Friday morning. Maybe it's the thought that Bodie and the Whitlocks are having a wonderful family Sunday while I'm left to stare at the wall of my house or the wall of the clubhouse. Alone.

Walking up the stone walkway, I push the doorbell and take a breath. My mom's expression tells me she's as shocked to see me as I am to be at her doorstep.

"Carter, is everything all right?" She gestures for me to come inside. I step over the threshold of the home I purchased for her years ago for the first time.

"No. Nothing is all right." I glance around the house that looks inviting but makes my skin crawl because I feel so out of place. "I want to know why."

"Why what?" Mom watches me with confusion. "Carter, come in, have a seat. We can sort out whatever is on your mind."

"You don't even know what's going on with me, so you have no clue what's on my mind. I live three miles from here, and I haven't seen you in over a year."

"You never accepted my invitation to visit, so I stopped trying." Her eyes drop to the floor. Avoiding. Hiding. That's what she does. Pretends like it never happened.

"Why did you let him do it? Why did you look the other way? Why didn't you get us the hell away from him?"

Her hand swipes at her cheek, but she never looks at me. "Fear. Of him. Of the unknown. Of everything. I wish a million times over I'd done things differently and got us both out of there." As her shaking hands swipe at her face, the only thing I feel is remorse and resentment for her, nothing that a son should feel towards his mother. Regret. She regrets it. But it's not enough. Action. That's what I needed. Safety. Security. Protection. Anything to get away from my father. And even if she should've done it, I can't help but pity her. She suffered at the hand of the bastard too. Only, I can't get past it enough to want her in my life on a regular basis. Forgiveness. That's what I need to give her. But I don't know how.

As I'm walking out, my mother calls my name. "Thank you, for doing for me what I couldn't do for you."

"No one deserves to be in his clutches." Walking out, I'm not sure what I wanted from her, but I knew damn well I wouldn't find it in this house. And I won't ever.

I shouldn't have come back.

This town. This team. It'll always be his.

Driving straight to the stadium, I pull into the lot driving a little faster than I should be even though I dread getting on the bus. Squealing to a stop, I see Dundee flagging me down.

"Lowe. Get your ass on this damn bus, now."

Why had I hoped it left without me? I step out of my truck, only my key fob and cell phone on me as I board the bus. The open seat next to Dundee is unfortunately the one I have to sit in. Which means this will be a long-ass ride.

"You should've left without me," is my response to Coach's bitching about me holding the team up.

"Is she worth your career, Lowe? Because that's what she's gonna cost you if you screw up this season."

"It's not about her." Or is it? I was fine until she brushed me off, lying to get rid of me. "She won't be waiting for me when I get off the bus this time."

He mumbles a few colorful words under his breath. "Then what the hell is it?" He glances around before lowering his voice. "Did Cash do something?"

"No. Not yet." But I know he's up to something. It's the calm before the storm with him. The moment he lets me think life is perfect and going great, he brings down the hammer to crush whatever good exists. Because the only thing the miserable bastard wants is for everyone else to be as miserable as him.

"He won't be able to do a damn thing to you if you keep your head on straight."

Too late.

29

AVERY

The bell rings, signaling the end of first period. E.J. makes his way over to my desk but not before yelling across the room that he'll catch up to his friend.

"Ms. W, I really need you to talk to your boy when he gets home tomorrow night. His last two starts haven't been all that great."

I know. I'd thought the same. When the coach walked to the mound for the second time in the same inning, I knew Carter couldn't get it together and was pulled from the game. "I'm not sure if he'll be around much."

"Did y'all break up?" he asks folding his arms over his chest as he nods.

"This conversation is not appropriate, Ernest. Get to your next class before you're late."

He huffs, mumbling something about legally changing his name the day he turns eighteen, then he walks out of the room.

Grabbing my phone, I look at the time. He won't be at the field yet. He'll probably be at the hotel. And E.J. didn't need to inform me of Carter's schedule—I can't help but follow it even when I try to avoid it. But what I really wish I could've avoided was watching last night's game, because I didn't recognize any part of the man I know.

It bugged me when Bodie made a comment about him needing to look at his cheat sheet a lot. Not only did I know that's not what he was doing, but I knew he was in a bad way because he looked at that card between every single pitch. He's definitely struggling with something, but it's not what pitch to throw, and my guess is it has something to do with Cash since he needed to constantly remind himself of why he was on the mound.

I hesitate but quickly type in the message and send it before I change my mind. Because I want to know.

Me: Are you okay?

Carter: Yes.

"Very convincing," I mutter.

Me: Then why did you look in your hat between every pitch?

I regret asking as soon as I send the message, but no matter what's going on (or not going on) between me and Carter, I want to know he's all right. And when the seconds tick by, turning into minutes, I finally realize he isn't going to respond. That worries me more than any answer he could've given.

30

CARTER

"Again," Coach commands.

Woodenly, I move up the bullpen mound, set up on the rubber, and throw the ball.

"Again," Dundee chirps.

Again, I mechanically throw the ball. There's no fire. No thought. I'm simply following an order. I stand and wait for either his approval or next instruction. He dismisses the catcher, leaving us alone in the bullpen. The sounds of the crowd arriving for the game can be heard, but it's not my day. Tomorrow is. And I know Dundee's level of concern is warranted. "There's no shame in standing down, kid."

"I'm ready," I reply flatly, which earns me an assessing look from Dundee.

"Your former team is in our house for a series, and you've been walking around here like a mindless zombie, and you want me to believe that you're ready to go?"

When I don't respond, he waves his hand, signaling for me to spill whatever he thinks I need to say. "I'm good."

He blows out a frustrated breath. "Yeah. Okay. Well, we'll see how ready you are tomorrow."

I walk into the clubhouse to shower and pull on the Coyote uniform.

"Hey, man. You good over there?" Brooks asks.

"Yeah." I am. I'm fine. I've done this for years. Pretending everything is fine is my thing. Even Avery said it. Only she knows the truth, and the fact that she noticed I was looking in my hat every pitch affirms that she sees through the façade, past all my bullshit, and it still doesn't make a fucking difference at the end of the day.

"How's Avery?"

"Wouldn't know," I retort, moving to sit in one of the leather chairs in the center of the room. I have no plan to move until it's time to head to the dugout. Every muscle in my body aches with tension, but it's not from the workout.

Brooks sits in the chair beside me, remaining quiet for a few as Gunner and some other guys ignore us and chipperly bounce around the room.

"What happened?" Brooks asks as I keep my eyes fixated on the ceiling.

"I guess she didn't like what she saw." And that was me.

"Do you really believe that load?" he asks as I look to him.

"I don't know what to believe." She pushed me away, then sent a stupid message. And it's a stupid message because now I know she's still watching my games. The person who didn't want shit to do with baseball or me, who ran at every chance, who doesn't want me around, is still watching me play. Was it all a bunch of bull?

"Me either."

Brooks remains next to me, a silent sentry, until it's time to head out to the field. Once we're in the dugout, I park my ass on the bench and don't move.

As I watch the Evergreens celebrate their victory in the visitors' dugout, I lock eyes with Mac, the only damn one to get a hit off of me in the last series. The thing is, he knows my skills better than most—the whole team, really, especially the pitching staff. It's harder to defeat someone when they can predict what you're going to do before you even know.

After changing, I make my way out to the stadium parking lot and see my former teammate propped against my truck.

"Carter Barlowe. Tough loss, man. Better luck tomorrow." Mac bends his elbow, swinging his arm around. "How's the arm, old man?"

"Get the hell outta here!" Dundee yells across the lot, causing Mac's satisfaction to grow, but he smirks and walks away. We all know it's a mind game, and anyone with half a brain can see that I'm struggling mentally. So the guys who know me, know I'm an easy target.

"Lowe," Dundee shouts as he walks over. I brace myself, sighing and putting my hands on my hips. I fully expect him to lecture me again, but he only tells me to call him if I want to go over the lineup before he walks off.

I don't need to review game strategy. I know those hitters and their stats inside and out. I know how they play, how they think. I know what they swing at and what scares them, where their hot and cold zones are. I know the pitches I need to throw. I just need to show up tomorrow and perform.

31

AVERY

"You ready?" Bodie stands at my door, grinning ear-to-ear, donning his Coyote jersey.

"No. Just watch the game with your brothers or something."

"I don't think Carter would appreciate me giving these seats away." Bodie holds up a white envelope, pulling out two tickets before shoving them back in the envelope and passing it to me.

"What is this?" I ask, reading the outside of the envelope.

See you at the game. —C.B.

"Why would he do this?" He's yet to reply to my message from four days ago but wants me at the game where he's throwing against his former team.

"Dunno. But chop, chop so we're not too late. These are some kick-ass seats." Bodie grabs the envelope from me, tucking it into his pocket as he pushes me towards my bedroom. "Do you even own a jersey? Or anything Coyote-blue?"

"No, of course not," I nearly scoff.

"Figures. How does the starting pitcher's girlfriend not even have his jersey?"

"Probably because I'm not his girlfriend." I walk into the kitchen, pour a second cup of coffee, and dig in my heels. I know Bodie isn't going to drop his quest of getting me to the game. And the last time we were in this situation, it tilted my world on its axis, sending Carter into my orbit where he doesn't belong. "I can't go."

"Yeah, you can. You have to. He sent these and wants you there. You really gonna turn him down after you've been sulking without him around?"

"I have not been sulking." *Damn it*. Why does Bodie play the annoying brother role so well?

"Sure, McPouty. Just throw something on, we can swing by and pick up a jersey for you."

"This is not a good idea."

"Last time didn't turn out so bad."

"Not sure everyone would agree with that statement, Bodie."

He pulls the envelope out of his pocket, pointing at the ink. "This tells me otherwise, McGloomy." He tucks it back into his pocket for safekeeping. "Now, get ready before traffic gets bad."

Is Carter testing me to see if I'll show and support him? Or show and read a book again? Definitely not taking that route again, especially since I actually want to see how the game plays out.

"Fine. But I'm not wearing a jersey." Especially his. I have to maintain some of my baseball indifference. I surely can't show up in his jersey, not with the uncertainty of whatever the hell is happening between us.

"Whatever you say, McDenial. Move your ass!"

32

CARTER

"Last chance, Lowe." Coach motions towards the field from the bullpen. The crowd roars around us. Even they know there's some beef there when I'm pitching on my new turf against my old team.

Fortunately, I woke up ready. Nothing is different, but this is what I do. This is my game. I go out there and get the job done. For me, not him. "I'm ready."

Dundee hesitates but nods for me to take the mound for my final warm-up. I'm good. I can do this. I need to redeem myself after my last two piss-poor performances. Because the only things worse than pitching for my dad's old team is not pitching at all. And Dundee has made clear that if I don't show the organization I'm good for the full season, I could be out next year. And so far, I'm not sure another team would pick me up.

Avery's face enters my mind, making me question whether I'd want to leave this town. There's still something deep inside me that hopes Brooks is right and I'm just full of bullshit and Avery and I aren't done.

My fingers tighten in my glove, my other lightly hitting

against the leather. Lynch stands up when I nod to him. *I'm ready, we're good.* And I know he trusts the look in my eye. He can always tell when I'm bullshitting. Dundee slaps my back, and Lynch and I make the long walk from the outfield to the dugout as the announcers introduce the lineup. It's game time. Right now, the only thing that matters is showing my old team that they gave up on me too soon and proving to my new team that they can count on me.

Five minutes later, the national anthem is over, and I take the mound to the screams and shouts of the home crowd. My home crowd.

I can do this. The first batter steps up as I look to Lynch, I nod to the signal, and deliver the pitch. Strike. *Yes. I can do this.*

When Lynch throws me the ball, my glove closes around it at the same moment I glance unconsciously to the stands behind the ump. Normally, I look unseeing at the crowd behind the plate. I'm not focused there. They don't faze me.

But a jolt of recognition zaps straight to my gut when my eyes meet hazel ones in the first row behind the plate, just to the right. *What the hell is Avery doing here?* She leans over, speaking closely into Bodie's ear. Glancing to the dugout as I make my way to the rubber, I get a confused look from Dundee. There's no way he's more confused than I am. Did he do this?

I set up for the pitch, making a concerted effort to avoid her eyes. The ball drills into Lynch's glove for another strike.

This is no different than any other game she's watched. It's fine. Taking a deep breath in, I force it out as I nod to the slider call and deliver a third strike. My eyes immediately find her smile as she claps and cheers with the fans around her. At least there's no damn book in her hand. I give her a slight smile as Lynch returns the ball to me.

I step to the top of the mound in preparation for the next batter when I see a person take the seat beside her.

My father.

There's panic on her face as she looks to me. What the hell is she doing sitting with my dad? He did this. But how would he know?

Lynch waves, getting my attention. As I accept his call, my body switches to autopilot. I wind up, but as I begin my forward momentum, my eyes can't help but look at him next to her, and as I release the ball, I know it's no good. Over-thrown, it's too high and out of the box, causing Lynch to run for it as the umpire calls ball one.

Dad sneers at me as he leans over, says something to Avery, then points to me.

"Lowe." Dundee is standing next to me. Where the hell did he come from? With his hand over his mouth to shield his lips from watchful eyes, he says, "What the hell is wrong?"

I lift my glove over my mouth. "He's here. Cash is sitting behind home. Get him out of here, and keep him the fuck away from Avery. Right now."

Dundee lets his shock show for a second but doesn't break eye contact with me. "I'll take care of it. But I need you to hold it together. Get through this inning or at least a few more pitches until I can get Murdock ready."

"I don't want to be relieved. I want him out of my sight and away from her."

"Give me a minute to get it handled, but keep your shit together, Carter. Don't give him exactly what he wants." Dundee lowers his hand and delivers an encouraging slap as he gives me a smile that I know is forced. He's just as pissed as I am. And he doesn't know the full extent of it. Goddamn, I want that bastard away from Avery.

Lynch calls a splitter that I shake off. When I finally agree to a call, I wind up and immediately find my father as I release the ball. Fuck. I'm losing it. The batter swings, getting a big enough piece to foul it. The next pitches are nowhere near where I intend them to be, and the count goes full. The hitter's final pitch is a ball that walks him to first base.

Mac steps up to bat as I watch an usher approach the row that Avery is seated in, leaning over to say something to my father. Mac tips the first pitch, sending it to left field for a foul. And I couldn't care less as I watch my father shrug off the usher and remain in his seat. The bastard won't leave. He knows precisely what he's doing.

Mac swings his bat around, squatting into his stance as he glances back. His smile taunts me. *Welcome to my head, asshole.* Now he's aware of exactly what's holding my attention—because this game sure as hell isn't. He flashes a grin as he winks, shouting, "Make Daddy proud, Carter."

The pain I feel in my elbow isn't real. The bone snapping happened years ago. But I still remember the moment because that's what I'd wanted to do—make my dad proud. I'd figured maybe he'd stop being a dickhead to me and my mom if I had a good game. Only, the opposite happened, it ignited the true beast I've since come to know.

Lynch motions a call and I mindlessly shake them off until Mac repeats the mocking encouragement to make Cash Barlowe proud. I don't bother with a nod to Lynch because I don't give a flying fuck what pitch he called. I have one target and it's shutting up the bastard who's mocking words are pulling out every vile memory that Cash Barlowe planted in my soul. When the ball releases from my hand, it misses Mac's head by inches as he ducks, dodging the pitch that would've hit him in the mouth if he hadn't anticipated the move.

Mac got the rise out of me that he wanted. Throwing his bat to the dirt, he heads my way. Lynch moves in front of him with a hand to his chest, he's a good dude trying to fight the good fight. But it won't stop this from happening. In my periphery, I note the benches clearing and the players rushing onto the field as I head straight for Mac.

I can't take out my anger on the one who deserves it, but Mac has had it coming. He shoves past Lynch, charging the mound, and I meet him halfway. Swinging my fist, I connect with his jaw. It should make me feel better. I figured it'd make me feel better, but all it does is haul up the recollection of when my knuckles last connected with another face— Cash Barlowe's when I'd finally gotten big enough to defend my mother after he went after her.

A swarm of bodies surrounds us, pulling me back as I fight to get free. But I don't want to get to Mac any longer. I want to get to my father and rip his head off, because whether Avery willingly engaged in the game he's playing or not, Cash Barlowe just unleashed a murderous rage in me that I've never felt before.

33

AVERY

I don't know what the hell is going on. The field has erupted into full-blown pandemonium. But that's not what has my head spinning, it's the man standing next to me, shaking his head in disappointment as we watch Carter be hauled off the field.

Cash leans over and I instantly shift away. Bodie is so starstruck that he fails to pick up on my vibe. The one that says *Stay the hell away from Cash Barlowe*. That's why Carter looked so surprised to see me. Cash was the *C* in C.B., not Carter. It makes perfect sense. Because I know Carter would never want his father here.

The crowd settles a bit as the players slowly make their way off the field while the umpires are gathered near first base. But the only person I want to see has disappeared out of sight. "I need to check on Carter."

Bodie gives me a crazy look as Cash motions for us to exit the row. "I'll show you where he is."

"No, that's all right."

"Avery," Bodie moves in front of me, allowing Cash to walk past. "Lead the way."

Why do I feel like I'm following a demon to my doom? But if he can get me to Carter, I'll go along while trying to keep my distance. Bodie is all but skipping alongside Cash as we walk down a small corridor. We come to a door and Cash punches numbers on a keypad, then holds the door open as Bodie and I slip inside before he follows.

It doesn't take long before I know I've found Carter. His shouting and cursing can be heard before I see him. When I finally do see him, his face is twisted in anger and increases tenfold when his eyes meet mine. In this second, I know showing up at the game today was a graver mistake than I ever could've envisioned. His livid glare darts to the man he hates most, standing beside me.

"Carter, please." I didn't realize until I begin to step towards him that the teammates on either side of him are holding him back. Physically restraining him. He looks feral, nearly out of control in that moment with his wild eyes and heaving chest. His hands sling around in the arms of the players shoving him back as he fights to get past them.

"What the fuck were you thinking? Did he put you up to it? Did he get you to do it?" he yells at me. Everyone else in the room is confused by his rant at me. But I don't pretend to misunderstand. He's accusing me of being in cahoots with Cash. And he's enraged. At me.

Carter focuses on his father. "Was this your plan all along? Was she your doing?"

I'm stunned that this, out of all scenarios, is the conclusion he's landed on. But the fury on his face, the rabid ire in his eyes, has transformed him. The man I never would've thought capable of causing me to flinch has me practically cowering. I've literally backed away from him slowly, but when his rage-filled eyes snap back to me, my ass hits a solid wall behind me as he rushes at me.

His body goes rigid as he halts his movements, his eyes on

me as his chest rises and falls quickly. I don't move; fear has frozen me in place. Logically, I know it's about his dad. But right now, he thinks everyone in this room is against him, and all of the faces bear various expressions of confusion and worry over being on the receiving end of his lashing.

Cash moves in front of me, and even if I were capable of understanding his words right now, I don't think I could hear them over the melee going on around us. Though my eyes are frozen on Carter's face, I'm aware of Dundee telling Cash to leave the area. Other players pull at Carter, but he stands unmoving, staring at me with a look of horror. I wish I knew what he was thinking but I can't even decide what I'm thinking other than I need to go. I knew I didn't belong here. I knew the first game. And I knew today. I shouldn't be here.

Spinning to flee, I pull open the door we'd just entered through. I hear Carter and Bodie shout my name, and almost at the same time, a grip captures my arm. Reflexively, I shrug away. Whipping my arm from the hand that's on me, I frantically turn to find Bodie.

Relieved, I beg, "Please, let's just go," and he quickly agrees without question as we rush down the corridor, straight to his truck. Once he's fired it up and we're halfway home, the awkward silence is finally interrupted. "Are you okay?"

"Yes," I lie, lacing my fingers after swiping at my cheek.

"What the hell happened back there?" Bodie asks.

And I give him an honest answer this time. "I have no idea."

From Carter to Cash, I can't wrap my mind around what happened because I can't get past Carter's anger being directed at me. And I can't get past the fact that he'd really think I'd form some kind of alliance with Cash after what he's shared with me, the truth that he's never shared with anyone.

34

CARTER

Me. She was scared of me. I know it. I've lived it. I recognized the fear in her eyes when she flinched away from me, afraid I was going to hit her. I've seen the exact same thing from my mom. And I never fathomed I'd see it in anyone's eyes who stood opposite me. But I saw it in Avery.

I click my phone, dialing her number again. It goes straight to voice mail. Fuck. I don't know what to think. I don't know if Cash had her play me. If she was a part of his sick joke. Or if she was simply caught in his vicious web. But one thing I know for sure: Her fear was real.

Dundee drops into the metal chair in front of me, leaning back as he folds his hands over his chest. A judging stare leveled on me. "Well, that went well."

I know he's trying to remain calm, and I also know him well enough to see he's about to boil over. And I deserve it.

"One job. You had one damn job, Lowe. Hold it together until I could handle the issue. Instead, you caused a bench-clearing fight. Congratulations."

My head drops, my eyes on my hands. "I tried." And I had.

But I lost my shit, and Cash won. No matter what he was after. He won because there was damage done.

"How's the hand?" He motions to my bloody knuckles that the team doctor has already examined. "You're lucky it's not broken."

I don't feel lucky, but he's right. I could've broken my hand, injured my arm, ended my career … all in a split second. But it's not what's pulling at my mind. My fingers rub across my sore knuckles as I squeeze tighter, the pain not enough to ease the torment in my mind. "She thought I was going to hit her."

"Were you?" he asks flatly.

My eyes snap to his. "Fuck no!" I fall back against the chair. "I'd never lay a hand on her. I was furious, but I'd *never* lay a hand on her. I needed her away from him. Even if she's part of his game, I need her away from him."

"Just go home, Carter. I'm trying to get your ass out of a jam here, but they don't know why you reacted like that, and I can't explain it."

"Don't tell them."

"I didn't plan on it. But there will be consequences. Between the dirty pitch that nearly took Mac's head off and the bench clearing, I'm guessing a suspension will be the least you're facing."

"Okay." I expected as much.

"Get your ass out of here." Dundee stands, shoving the chair back with a frustrated kick.

"Coach." I take a second before looking to him. "I'm sorry."

"Me too. I should've let you deck the bastard." Dundee doesn't like Cash any more than I do. It's one of the reasons we clicked right away and the reason I'd shared the truth with him. I'd needed him to understand what this team and all the baggage that comes with it means to me. Not that it had done any good.

I head to my locker and quickly change, hearing the game back in progress. I need to find Avery. One way or another, I need to see her. I'm about to leave when I hear Brooks call my name. "I need to speak with you."

"Not now." I hate brushing him off, but I need to get to Avery.

"She wasn't in on it."

I stop at his words. How would he know anything about what's going on in my mind? And also, what the hell is he doing in the clubhouse and not on the field?

"Cash knew he could use her to push your buttons. He's been keeping tabs on you." Brooks pauses then drops the news that I never saw coming. "Cash had me keeping tabs on you."

"What the hell are you talking about?" My anger increases with each word, but confusion is the only thing I can express as I look to my teammate.

"Why else would a rookie get such a good deal? He placed me here with the condition of keeping tabs on you ... and I have a feeling he's just getting started."

I surge forward, grab his jersey, and slam him against the wall. "Why the fuck would you do that?"

"Because I wanted to play. But once I figured out that he wasn't just being a supportive dad who wanted to reconnect with his son, I backed out. He pushed me for information on Avery, and when I wouldn't provide what he wanted, he had me benched. Cash might not play for this team, but he still pulls the strings."

No. He can't mean what I think he's getting at.

"Think about it. Why else would a team take a chance on a guy who just had surgery, not knowing how successful it was or how well you'd recover unless someone wanted you here?"

"You're lying."

"I'm sorry, I shouldn't have agreed to any of this shit. None of it is worth it and we have no control."

My finger releases the fabric of his jersey, the same fabric I just removed from my back. And the only reason we're both wearing it is because of my father's doing? Brooks is telling me Cash had the team give me a contract?

Instead of heading out of the stadium, I head for the dugout. Dundee spots me and steps out of sight of the crowd, leading me back into the tunnel. "Lowe, you can't—"

"Is it true?"

He gives me a confused look before recognition dawns on his face. "Carter."

"I was only signed because of him? And you knew about it?"

Dundee takes a few steps, stopping as his back hits the cinder block wall, propping up in a defeated pose that I feel in every part of my being as I stand in front of him. "Cash wanted you here, and the front office agreed to a year. If you proved yourself, they said they would keep you around for your talent. That's why I've been pushing you. I needed you to show them you *deserve* to be on this team. You're a talented player, which has not one thing to do with that piece of shit."

This can't be real. All the work I put in. All the time I spent proving myself, only to have him get me the contract. I thought the organization had faith in me. I thought I earned my place in this sport. "How many times has he pulled strings behind the scenes, and I didn't know about it?"

"Just this. He only has pull in this organization. From what I hear, he has some damning info on some higher-up."

Of course he'd blackmail Coyote brass and employ dirty

methods to get his way. Anything at any cost, no matter who it hurts. "I'm done. With all of it. The team. The league. The sport. And everything linked to my father."

"No, Lowe, that's what he wants."

"Well, he's finally getting it—exactly what he's always wanted—and he didn't even have to break my arm this time." I pivot, walking out to my truck.

I don't know where I'm going, but I need to get away from the stadium. Away from the cheering and adoration. Away from the lights and smells. Because all of it is one big Cash Barlowe spectacle.

35

AVERY

"Have you heard from Carter at all?" Bodie asks the question I knew was coming.

"No." And not from lack of trying, only my calls went straight to a generic message that the mailbox was full. I'd debated even calling for hours after running out of there yesterday. But in the end, my worry for him and what his dad stirred up was greater than anything else. Cash got to him like *that*.

Bodie pulls to a stop in front of my parents' home. I'd debated skipping lunch today, but I didn't want to explain to Mom why I wouldn't be here. And I didn't want to sit at home alone any longer. Especially after getting the crazy idea of driving to Carter's house. If his phone is shut off, he's wanting to be left alone. He'd probably be at the field right now anyway since there's a game coming up.

"I'm sure he'll come around." Bodie tries to sound positive as he bails out of his truck, and I follow behind as we make our way into the house. The usual delicious aroma of home cooking fills the air as I take in the comforting scent, finding my mom in the kitchen as she wraps me in a warm embrace.

She doesn't say anything but her sympathetic expression assures me that she knows about what took place at the game yesterday.

"Hey, hey," Rhett calls out as he enters the kitchen, glancing between me and Bodie. "How's lover boy's hand? While that scuffle was entertaining as hell, he can't be risking his moneymaker like that."

Bodie steps in front of me, shielding my brother's mocking face as he tells Rhett to leave me alone. The teasing isn't what's bothering me, it's the fact that I don't know what's going on with Carter.

Attempting to shift my focus, I move to help Mom as my phone chimes with a message from Dad. So much for shifting my focus.

"What's wrong?" Bodie asks as I look up to him.

"My dad asked if I'd go up to the store because someone's there to see me."

"I'll go with you." Bodie follows me as I head to the door.

"Me too. I really want to hear this." Rhett calls out, no doubt with the same assumption I have. It's Carter.

"No. You stay here." I'm unsettled enough without my little brother pestering me.

"Fine." Rhett quips, walking out of the room in much the same manner as Finn does right before throwing a hissy fit when he doesn't get his way.

The gravel crunching under our shoes is the only sound as Bodie and I quickly make our way to the store to find Dad and my visitor. I was partly right, there's a Barlowe here to see me, but it's not Carter. The sight of Cash sends nothing but disdain through me. I watch him smile at my dad before looking to where Bodie and I stand wordlessly.

"Avery, Mr. Barlowe stopped by to check on you." Dad has a little less warmth in his voice than normal. I'm glad my dad isn't acting starstruck by the washed-up athlete because he's not someone who should be idolized, he's someone who should be exiled.

"It's the least I could do after the trouble my son caused yesterday. You ran off in such turmoil, I was worried about you." Most would mistake him for sincere, but I know the truth, and I loathe the satisfaction in his voice. "Do you mind if we chat privately for a moment?"

"Avery." Bodie moves closer to me.

"I'll meet you back at the house." My instructions don't please Bodie. He's not in the know, but he's smart enough to discern something went down yesterday between Cash and Carter that goes deeper than what it seemed.

"I'll wait outside for you." Bodie begrudgingly steps away from me.

Dad tells Cash it was nice to meet him, extending a hand as they share a friendly shake that makes me want to pry the elder Barlowe's fingers from my dad's.

We stand in the middle of the store, Cash glances around before he finally breaks the tension-ridden quiet. "It's a nice business your father has built here."

"You sent the tickets. You wanted me at the game, not Carter."

He lets out a soft chuckle, his hand rubbing across his mouth, there's no hiding the amusement in his smile. "I just wanted to meet the lady who was the first to capture my son's attention. It's not an easy feat. Trust me."

I don't trust anything about this piece of shit. And I can't explain the irrational anger that floods me as he leisurely takes stock of my family's store. "You should go."

Cash doesn't seem insulted, but amused, at my statement. "I will. But first, I'd like to offer you a little proposition."

"Not interested."

He stops, picking up an item, examining it like he plans to purchase it. "You haven't even heard my proposal. And with how things have been going between you and Carter, I'd suggest you at least hear me out."

How would he know anything about what's going on between me and Carter? It's not like Carter calls his dad for friendly chats and life updates.

"I really didn't think you'd get to him so fast. I figured he could at least make it through an inning or two without losing concentration. A good pitcher wouldn't have been distracted in the least. A weak mind has always been Carter's downfall. I never let anything impede my objective."

There's nothing good about this vile monster in front of me. Of all people to call weak-minded, Carter is the least of them. It's more than evident he has no clue who his son actually is. "I doubt there's much that could *impede* a man who'd break his ten-year-old's arm out of jealousy."

Shock is evident in his expression before he quickly recovers. "The fact that you know that tells me everything I need to know. So, here's my offer. I need Carter on the field through the end of this season. He'll be on suspension for that stunt yesterday, but I've received word that he doesn't plan to return to the team after discovering some contract issues."

Stupidly, I ask the only question in my mind. "Why do you give a shit if he plays or not? Especially after what you orchestrated yesterday to get him out of the game?"

"My son wants to prove to the world he is a better player than me. I set the stage, but he failed again." He doesn't hide his pleasure. Like a twisted bastard. "But if he doesn't play, he'll never know exactly how useless and pathetic his attempt to overshadow me was. So, here's my offer: Keep him here in Canaan Falls, playing for the season, and you'll be substantially compensated at the end of the season."

"You really need to leave. Now." What the hell is wrong

with this delusional man? He really thinks I'll help him manipulate Carter when I know the truth?

"My former alliance said you couldn't be bought. But I wasn't convinced. My mistake. But you have to know this doesn't end well for you and Carter, not when the two of you clash at every turn with your different … lifestyle choices." He takes a slow glance around the store, doing an assessment of my casual T-shirt and shorts. "How's the teaching job going? I have a few buddies on the school board. I believe they have something to do with funding … and layoffs."

It's a threat. Clear as day. And he's not done.

"Maybe I can do some publicity for this place. It would bring in more than that silly signing Carter arranged. Really put this place on the map." His smile fades as he glares at me. "Or remove it completely. I can be an influential man within this community. I'd hate for the business your father built to be run into the ground. One bad experience can really put a damper on a small business."

He wants to screw with my job, okay. My parents' livelihood? Fuck no.

"My father built this place from the ground up alongside my mother. He knows every customer's name and what they shop for during what season, down to the variety of roses they prefer. And they know the man he is. So, no one will ever believe your bullshit lies about him or this place."

"Are you willing to risk all this?" He waves around, taking a step towards me. "Over a silly fling that won't last either way. Take the payday and help me."

The man that wants to be seen as intimidating appears as nothing but a weak, pathetic asshole in front of me. "You knew it then, and you know it now—Carter is a better player than you on the field and a better man off the field. And I will not take any part in your hideous plan. And I won't stand for you being in his life. So, take your threats and shove them up your ass. And just know, if you try to hurt him or my family, I won't hesitate to tell your adoring public the truth about the bastard you are off the field."

His laugher fills the room. "Even if anyone would believe your claims, you'd never do that to Carter. He trusted you with a secret that he's kept hidden for years. He'd never speak to you again. I wouldn't be the monster anymore, you would. And you'll be on the losing end once again."

What a cocksure asshat. Taking a step forward, I look at him through narrowed eyes because I mean every word of what I say. "I've dealt with scarier bullies than you in my classroom on a good day. So, be sure that you don't mind every single person in this city knowing what a brutally sadistic father you were because I will follow through on my threat. I don't care if Carter never speaks to me again. I will do whatever necessary to keep him out of your grasp and as far away from your sorry ass as possible." Shit, I hope it doesn't come to that, but I can't let this man think he has any power over me or Carter, because that's what he thrives on. And after seeing Carter spiral out of control at the game, Cash can't get wind of the damage he can really do. But he probably already knows.

"My offer stands. Either way, he'll end up being his own undoing. He always has been just like his weak-willed mother." With that, he arrogantly strolls out.

My hand automatically reaches out, bracing myself on the wood counter as I try to understand what just happened and figure out what to do. Carter might not want to answer my calls, but I have to warn him about what his father is up to. I need to reach someone who cares enough to keep Cash as far away from Carter as possible. If he's blindsided, it'll be even worse, and Cash Barlowe will not be Carter's undoing. He can't be. For Carter's sake.

CARTER

Whoever is ringing the doorbell isn't going away. What I really want to know is how the hell they bypassed the gate that is supposed to keep people out in the first place. And being that less than a handful of people have the code, no one should be ringing my damn doorbell.

As I pull open the front door, Dundee's pissy stare confirms it's one of the few in possession of the gate code.

"About damn time, Lowe." Dundee pushes past me, stepping into my house.

"Come on in." My hand slings the door closed behind him. *Here it comes.*

"The league reached a decision. Ten-game suspension and a hefty fine. Then, I expect to see your stubborn ass back on the field."

"Not gonna happen." I walk to the formal living room and drop onto the stiff leather sofa. "Shouldn't you be there now, *Coach?*" It's still early in the morning, but Dundee is usually there before most.

Dundee stands in front of me with his disapproving and

furious gawk aimed at me. "I would be if it weren't for having to track down your miserable ass."

"Well, message delivered. My agent knows the deal. He'll be in touch with the team." Joe was less than thrilled at the news, but I have a feeling it was more to do with his pay cut than worrying about the contract I'm under with the Coyotes. I couldn't give a shit. I told him whatever had to be done, do it. I don't care what it costs me, I have to get out of the contract that my father arranged.

"That easy, huh?" Dundee takes an assessment of me. His disapproval clear but he keeps a flat tone.

What part of this is easy? None of it feels easy.

Coach takes a deliberate step forward. "Never pegged you for a quitter."

My fury grows but I try to remain calm on the outside. "There's a difference between quitting and being done with the bullshit."

"The only thing that's bullshit is you letting Cash Barlowe influence the choices you make about your career. All those years you worked your ass off, down the drain."

"You should've told me."

"Why? So, you could act exactly like this?" He gestures to me before slinging his hand in the air. "It's one season. I saw your talent and knew you were destined to be ten times the player your father ever was. And I wanted it to be under my watch. I just needed to get you to prove yourself to the team, so they'd keep you here. That's when I was going to tell you. After you knew this was *your* team because it's where you should be."

"It's his team. It'll always be. That much is clear."

"You have a choice. Step up and play the damn game. Or stand down and play his. Pick wisely, Carter, because you deserve better than the shitty cards Cash has dealt you time and time again."

"I'm done." I repeat the words, trying to block out Dundee's. How can I step onto that field knowing the sole reason I'm there is because of my father?

His head drops as he shakes it. "You're gonna regret it." Just before he reaches the door, he turns to look at me. "I had a curious visitor at the stadium yesterday."

"Okay."

"She wanted to warn me about Cash. She said he has some kind of plan to ruin your career, and she was worried about you. Avery cared enough about you that she waited outside the gate, hollering at every person she saw until someone escorted her back to my office. And you can't get off the damn couch to save yourself."

My eyes focus straight ahead on the wall. "Was she okay?"

"Ask her yourself."

The door slams, echoing through the empty house, and that only serves to make me feel worse by the second.

I want to ask her. I want to get off the couch. I want to save myself. But the only thing I can see is my father's wicked face behind the plate where I started the first fight I've ever had on the field—reminding me that I'm not in control of myself.

37

AVERY

"You can totally bail on me." Bodie pulls my attention from the familiar landscape as I ride shotgun to his brother's wedding.

I can't say I hadn't thought about bailing. After a long, worrisome week of no word from Carter—and thankfully nothing out of Cash—I'm exhausted. But I'd promised Bodie and since it's Greg (the brother I adore, not the one who ripped my heart out), I really do want to go.

"Yeah. I should. But I can't bail on your brother."

"Oh, so this is all for him?" Bodie laughs, waving over the length of me. "Here I thought you got all dolled up for me." His grin stretches wide as he reaches over to grab my hand. "You look beautiful, Avery."

"Thanks." I glance out the window, my free hand smoothing down the soft fabric of my dress.

Oddly, Bodie remains quiet for the remainder of the ride. Once he pulls to a stop in the parking lot, I glance around, noting we are super early since he has to take pictures. He hurries around the hood, shutting the passenger door as I rub my hands over my already smooth dress, eyes turned to the ground.

"Avery." Bodie's soft tone pulls my eyes to him as he steps forward, swiping his hand across my exposed back where the dress is lined in lace. There's a look of remorse on his face as he pulls me into his embrace. "He'll come around."

"I'm fine."

"No lying to your best friend." He releases me, taking my hand in his as we start to walk into the venue. "But I really believe he'll come around. He has a lot going on right now. With the suspension and fallout from the game, I'm sure he's trying to get everything straight."

"Yeah. That's probably it." I agree because I want to think he's staying away and avoiding my calls for that reason and not because he doesn't want to see me.

"Besides, he'd be a real dumbass to not see what a wonderful woman you are."

"Thanks." My best friend is really trying to pull me out of my funky mood, so I resolve to do my best to enjoy the event. I fix a smile on my face as we're greeted by Bodie's family, including the brother I do my best to avoid. As soon as Russell makes eye contact and takes a step in my direction, Bodie says something to him, and I take the opportunity to pivot and find a place to hang out while they snap some pictures.

During the gorgeous ceremony, I tell myself I'm just wrapped up in the moment, but the truth is, I realize how much I want this. Not the wedding, not the showy day, just someone to spend the rest of my life with. And of all people, Carter enters my mind. Cash's cruel words soon follow as I shake it all out of my head. There's no point dwelling on something I have absolutely no control over.

Once the ceremony is over, the wedding guests are shuffled into the reception area where Bodie soon joins me dancing, laughing, and having a wonderful time. And it's when I'm spinning out of a turn from Bodie that I spot someone else.

Carter.

He's standing at the edge of the room, hands tucked into the pockets of his jeans. The sleeves of his button-down are rolled up, exposing his forearms as he stands casually, like he's supposed to be here. Which is wrong. He shouldn't be here. But damn, I'm glad he is. Only I can't decipher the look on his face.

Bodie soon realizes I've stopped participating in the dance and looks to where my gaze is fixated, no doubt spotting who I'm seeing. He looks just as surprised, leaning over to whisper, "Told you he'd come around."

With that, he takes my hand, walking me to where Carter is standing. Unfortunately, my brother, who I'm certain wasn't on the guest list, is standing beside him.

"Ta-da," Rhett says, gesturing to Carter, whose eyes are locked with mine.

"What are you doing here?"

"Stupid question." Rhett laughs, slapping Carter on the back. "But now that I'm here, I'd better grab some grub." He walks away, pointing his fingers at me. "You're welcome."

I might be thankful he brought Carter here but that won't stop me from telling him what a buttface he is later.

"Carter Barlowe."

Shit. Russell steps next to Bodie, who is already shoving him away. After a few choice words and redirection, Bodie gets the douchebag away, giving me an encouraging nod as he follows his brother.

"I should hire Bodie as my bodyguard." Carter glances across the room to where Bodie is in a heated conversation with his idiotic brother.

"He was protecting me." I admit as Carter turns his attention to me. "History. That's it. A dumb jock football player who used me and almost cost me my best friend."

"Ah," Carter nods, looking back to feuding brothers. "Well, guess I have something else to thank Bodie for." He returns his gaze to me. "You look stunning, Avery."

Okay. This was not something I ever pictured happening. "What are you doing here?"

"I went to see you at your place, but you weren't there, so I went to your parents' place. Your dad told me about the wedding and had Rhett show me the way over."

Out of all the people, he sent him with Rhett. Ugh, but I'll take it.

"Can we go somewhere and talk?"

"I tried. I've been trying to call you all week," I stupidly admit.

Carter takes a deliberate step forward, moving just in front of me. "I picked up the phone a million times. To answer, to call, to text, but what I had to say didn't feel right coming through a phone. And I needed to see you when I said it. I'm so sorry, Avery. I'm sorry I scared you. I wasn't going to touch—I'd *never* lay a finger on you. I just wanted to get you away from my father. I lost it. It made me crazy that he was so close to you." He lets out a frustrated breath, stepping forward as he brings his hand up, sliding his palm along the side of my neck, his fingers lightly gripping as his lips move near mine. "I'm so sorry, Avery."

My arms come up, wrapping around his neck as he places a tender kiss on my lips before leaning back. "Will you come somewhere with me?"

It's not even a question, because I'm pretty sure I'd follow him anywhere he'd want to go, but I'm not ready to admit that to him just yet. So I simply nod my head, and he leads me away.

When I look back, I see a triumphant smile on Bodie's face as he mouths, "I told you so."

Yes, he did. And I'm sure he'll remind me of such a few more times, but I can't celebrate quite yet because as steady as Carter's hand is in mine, I know our feet are on shaky ground. And I fear the damage Cash has already done will have a bigger hold on Carter than he can resist. It's hard not to wonder what lurks around the corner when dealing with a demented man hell-bent on hurting his son.

38

AVERY

Out of all the places Carter drives, it's to the ballpark. Most of the parking lot is empty, until Carter steers into the private area for the players where there are vehicles lined around.

"Should we be here?" I ask when Carter pulls open the passenger door, holding his hand out to me.

"Yeah. We're good."

Sliding off the seat, I take his hand as he leads me through a door and down a long corridor before we eventually make our way onto the field.

"It's so different." My eyes search the dimly lit stadium, the calm and quiet making it seem like a different place, but it feels comforting.

"The team's in Seattle. Yesterday should've been my day to pitch." His posture tenses a little before he clasps his hand around mine, leading me to the dugout. "The first game I attended, I was so excited that I got away from my mom and ran into the dugout right before the game was about to start. Dad laughed it off when he led me back to my mom, but later that night, she had a bruised eye and a busted lip. I didn't understand it until I was older, but he'd waited until we were home to react. That's what he would do. He'd put on the show, hold in his anger, then react when no one was watching."

His hand releases mine, moving to rub through his hair, pulling at the locks. He sits on the bench before his hands drop, landing between his legs, and I sit beside him. "There's nowhere in this place where I don't see him. Nothing that hasn't been tarnished." Carter pushes up, pacing up the steps to the edge of the dugout. Leaning back against the railing, he looks over the roof into the stands. "Until you."

He moves back down the steps, dropping to his knees in front of me. His hands move to my sides, gripping my hips. "All I see when I look behind this dugout is a beautiful woman with her nose in a book and not the least bit interested in me." Damn, how times have changed because he holds my full interest now as he leans forward, brushing a tender kiss on my mouth. "Thank you."

He kisses me—everything about it is tender and gentle— then he pulls back, moving to sit on the bench beside me. "When I saw him next to you, I lost my mind. The only good memory I had to cling to—he stole it from me, and I wasn't sure if he hadn't set the whole thing up. I know you better than to accuse you of something like that, but the vile evilness he's implanted in my brain … it makes me think the absolute worse of everyone. I'm sorry—"

"No. Stop apologizing." I pause for a second, only to debate what to say. Though I'm scared it will send him spiraling, I need to make sure he got the message from his coach. "Your father has something planned. I don't know what it is. But he wants to ruin your career in a very public way."

"I know. He arranged it." Carter waves his hand around, his eyes scanning the stadium. "He did all of it. He's the reason the team wanted me. The reason they signed me not knowing if I'd ever pitch again. I should've known a washed-up player who'd just had surgery doesn't get deals like that, not without a price."

I turn on the bench to look fully at him. "I might not know baseball, but I know the man I've seen on this field isn't a washed-up player. He's a man who was given an opportunity to prove he's a great pitcher, despite just having surgery. Cash really thought you wouldn't show him up, but you came back even stronger, because that's who you are. I know that and he knows that. And it's the reason he's resorting to dirty plays to get what he wants, because he can't do it fairly."

Carter remains silent for a few seconds before saying, "How do I get through a game knowing I'm only here because of him?"

"He might be the reason you came here, but it's your choice to stay. And it's your choice to call the pitches. It's up to you how you play, and how you walk off the field, and what you do behind closed doors afterwards. He might be the asshole who pulled the strings to get you out on this field, but he can't make you something you're not."

His head falls back, his eyes closing as he rubs his hands over his face. "I can't quit. But I can't finish this season out knowing it was him. I don't know what to do."

"You show up. You take it one game at a time. You do what you're trained to do. Put him out of your mind, and do it for you, not him."

"You can't use my words against me." Carter lets out a slight laugh that brings me a heaping amount of relief.

"That's not in my rule book." I return the light tone, hoping he can begin to chip away at unloading the demons he's carried with him for so long as he glances around the field. "So, here's another reminder of your words. What's most important to you?"

His eyes search mine, giving me a puzzled expression.

"To be on the mound," I remind him. "That's what you wanted. That was your goal. To play. Don't let him take away your dream."

Reaching over, Carter grips my sides, half lifting, half pulling me onto his lap to straddle him. His palms smooth up the bare skin of my thighs as his hands slip under my dress, squeezing my legs before he removes one to cup my cheek. He leans in for a kiss, feathering his lips over mine. "Dreams change."

I don't want to examine his words or take away from the moment as he kisses me, making another memory for the both of us.

39

CARTER

This is the first time I've ever been suspended. And while the reasoning bothers me, I'm not complaining about the unorthodox break. Because even with the sun peeking through the windows and Avery's nude body draped over mine, I know I won't have to let her go to get to the field. I can also hide away from what I don't want to face for a while longer. Because as much as I hear Dundee's encouragement and believe Avery's words, I still feel my father's grip.

My hand glides up her back as she nestles closer, letting out a sigh. "I have to start getting ready."

"Sunday Whitlock family lunch?" I ask already knowing it's an inflexible part of her day but one I finally can be a part of instead of watching her and Bodie head off without me. "Mind if I join? Not that it matters since I have an open invitation from your mom and all."

"Yeah, yeah." She playfully slaps my chest as she moves to roll off of me.

Grasping her wrist, I pull her flush to my chest. "Are we good, Avery?"

A grin covers her face as she says, "I am. And you'd better be after that blow."

Her sexy look tangles up with the memories of us last night, ensuring she's not using the term in a sports-related context. And I can't stop looking at her gorgeous, teasing smile.

"I'll have to tell Coach you give way better blows than he does."

Her hand slaps against my chest, harder this time, her eyes widening in shock. "You'd better not, Carter."

I squeeze her ass, holding her to me. "I'll think about it."

Stepping into the kitchen, her mother greets us with a warm embrace, and Finn wastes no time running to jump into Avery's arms. *I know the feeling, buddy.* She's amazing. And I realized how far under her spell I am when she said not to let my father take my dream away, because now that includes her.

"Carter," Rhett hollers, "you're here." His voice is a little bit too shocked considering he's the one who brought me to Avery at the wedding last night.

Bodie adds to the noisy kitchen as he shouts across the room. Looking to me, he smiles and lifts his chin in greeting. And I'm glad to return his smile. I'd hoped he wouldn't be bothered by my presence, especially after I saw him with her on the dance floor. For a second, I'd questioned if she was happier without me. It sure had looked like it as she laughed and twirled around the dance floor with Bodie. But I need her. I want her. And it feels like we might have a chance at staying on that track.

Everyone finds a spot at the table, and I sit next to Avery and across from Rhett, who I'm getting strange vibes and looks from. It's not something that I'm unused to. But I hope he can get used to me dating his sister because I'm not going anywhere.

Looking around the table, I take in the chatter, everyone talking to each other whether they are across the table or across the room, but it's the best sound ever. The meals I was used to having were alone in my room or at an empty table.

"Hey, you all right?" Avery asks nudging me. "I know they're a lot to take in."

"They're perfect." I smile, leaning over to place a quick kiss on her cheek as we resume our meal until there's a knock on the door. Lyle stands, making his way there. Seconds later, I hear my agent's voice. *What the hell?*

Rising from the table, I'm met with Joe's agitated expression as he walks in the room, his phone in hand. "I've been trying to call you all morning."

"A little busy."

"Yeah, well. Me too. We really need to talk about a damn good plan to get in front of this."

He slaps his phone against my palm, and I look to the screen. Clicking the button, a video plays. Avery and my father stand in what I recognize as the Whitlock's feed store, and when the audio starts playing, my father's voice chills me to the bone. What the hell is he doing talking to her? My eyes flick up to see Avery's look of shock. I register it but am laser focused on what's going on in the video.

Next to me, Avery mutters something and explodes out of her chair but remains standing next to me. Raised voices talking over each other surround me, but I zone in on the exchange playing out on Joe's phone. I watch her tell my father she'll expose him even if it hurts me if only to keep him away.

"Carter." Her voice sounds desperate, pleading as she tries to get the phone out of my hand. I release it, having seen enough, but the conversation continues to replay in my mind.

Joe says, "We need a game plan. If you want to spin it in your favor we can. But my source at Channel Twelve said it's set to air on tomorrow morning's broadcast."

"No, no, no," Avery says, looking at the phone. Her hands shake as she clicks against the phone's screen. "How did they get this? We were alone. There wasn't anyone else in the store." Her body goes rigid, then her glare whips to a confused Bodie. "You were there."

"You can't be serious." He shakes his head, holding up his hands. "I wouldn't do that to you, Avery."

"You were the only one there!" she shrieks, waving the phone in the air.

Objectively speaking, Bodie remains way too calm in the face of his best friend's hysterics. But I can't say much since I'm watching everything play out in silence while my head grasps the full gravity of what I just saw.

"No, I wasn't. Your dad was there."

"Really? You're gonna accuse my dad?" Avery yells leaning across the table to get in Bodie's face until Rhett speaks up.

"It's not his fault," Rhett says.

"Stay out of this." Avery moves like lightning out from her spot beside me and around the end of the table, presumably to get to Bodie. But Rhett blocks her, meeting her halfway.

"I did it." His eyes quickly dart to mine. "I took the video."

"What?" she breathes, her hand gripping the phone as her arm drops to her side. "Why would you do that? How could you do this?"

"It was an accident. I was excited to see Cash in our store, so I wanted to take a quick video, until I heard what you were saying. I didn't know it was gonna get leaked. I sent it to a few of my buddies, but they promised not to do anything with it. We just couldn't believe what a douche Cash really is." He gives me a pitying look and it makes my stomach roll. I don't want this out there. But it's too late.

"Yes. Everyone will know," Joe retorts. "My source said they dug up a photo of yours at age ten when your arm was in a cast, and it's not that hard to put two and two together."

Avery looks to me. "I'm so sorry. I never should've said those things." She rambles apologies to me and threats to her brother as her anger rises until she finally turns to face Rhett. "I'm gonna kill you." The phone slings out of her hand, whipping across the room to where Rhett has distanced himself. He sidesteps and ducks in time for the phone to shatter against the wall in an impressive show of force, barely missing him. Enraged, whether from missing the intended target or just in general at her brother, she charges. Her hands reach for him, but Bodie holds her back while I still stand stupidly in a disorienting haze.

"That was my phone," Joe states bluntly, shaking his head way too calmly given all the chaos around us.

All I see is Avery. Her face. Her smile. Her anger. All I hear are her words. Her outrage. Her venom. Finally snapping out of my daze, I step near her, reach forward, grasp her neck in my hand, and bring my mouth to hers. Kissing her fervently, I wedge between her and Bodie, my body pressing against hers, aligning us in our perfect way. She doesn't respond for a moment, a shocked gasp comes from her lips, then she catches up and kisses me back.

Easing back slightly, I smile against her lips. "Thank you."

She looks completely dumbfounded as she stares up at me, brow scrunched.

"You were protecting me. And at any cost." I've witnessed the fierce side of this quiet woman who sits with her nose in a book. She may have run away from me in the beginning and drives me insane with passion in the present, but she stood up to my father. For me. Willing to lose everything in order to keep him away from me and protect me. Something no one, not even my own mother, has ever been willing to do for me.

"I don't understand. Why aren't you mad? Everybody is gonna know." Her arms contract around my waist gripping me tightly, and I wrap mine around her to hold her against me.

"It'll be okay." It has to be.

"I'm sorry—" I shake off Rhett's apology.

It doesn't matter what, how, or who—it's done. And I don't blame anyone in this room. The only one responsible for what's to come is the man who's hidden his true self from the world. And maybe I'm partly to blame, because I've hidden it for him too.

AVERY

To say family lunch didn't go well would be a vast understatement. But even more surprising is Carter's calm, even relaxed, demeanor. How is he not livid about the news that will be shared with the world in the morning? The secrets he's kept to himself so long are being revealed because I have a big mouth and my idiotic brother is a nosy fool with a damn camera phone.

"I'm so sorry, Carter. Really."

"Would you have told anyone had he made a move?"

"I was hoping I'd never have to decide, but I can tell you that I wasn't going to let him hurt you or my family."

His hand clasps mine, bringing my knuckles to his mouth before resting our hands on the console between us.

"What are you going to do?"

"Exactly what I told Joe. We have no comment right now. We're gonna let the story play out until I decide if and when I want to address it. Joe still has hopes of squashing it with some other story. Or someone doing something that will catch more attention."

"Yeah. Let's hope."

"Never know."

He's still too calm. I hear his words, believe he isn't angry, but I don't get it. "I'm sorry. This is still my fault."

"Well, then I guess you owe me," he says with a joking tone, and now I worry where this is going. "I demand you play hooky tomorrow. I want you all to myself for the entire day so we can hide away and forget all about everything."

That does sound good even if taking a day off again so soon, and last minute, doesn't sit well. The news will break tomorrow morning and the classroom isn't where I want to be. "Deal. And I need to get Joe another phone to replace his broken one."

"Nah, the longer he doesn't have a phone, the better. Don't worry, I'll take care of it."

I don't like it, but I give in, mainly out of exhaustion, both physically and mentally.

Once we're back at my place, we settle in to watch a movie. Comfortable and cozy, I wish we could shut the world away just a little bit longer.

41

CARTER

"Well, well. Look who's graced us with his presence after all," Coach Dundee quips, stepping into the bullpen as I release another pitch before looking to him. "Here a little early aren't we, Lowe?"

I haven't been late to a practice since my suspension was lifted, but Dundee hasn't missed the chance to bust my balls at every opportunity. And it's refreshing because I know what his intentions are and where his loyalty lies, just as I know where Avery's are. I know I have two people in my corner who are looking out for my best interests.

"So, what are we going to do tomorrow if Cash shows his stupid ass?"

"I'm good. He won't get to me again."

"No comment, right?" Dundee repeats my stance on the topic that the news stations have reported on for a week.

Thankfully, it hasn't inundated the headlines, it's only stirred up the die-hard fans. Avery had a difficult time with the last week of school with a few reporters who waited for her in the parking lot, but she did wonderful. Keeping her cool, she avoided the issue. Thankfully, it was the final week of the school year, so she'll be at the feed store for the summer. I don't worry about anyone hounding her there because I know her dad will make sure to keep the vultures prying for a juicy story away. Though, I'd told her to speak to them if she wanted to. It happened to me, but I'd also brought her into it, so if she feels the need to say something, I'll support her decision because I know it'll be made with our best interest at heart.

With tomorrow being my first start in weeks, I was on edge, but when she agreed to come to the game, a weight was lifted. Cash used her to get to me because he knew she must be special, and I allowed him to make me question someone I care for deeply. It won't happen again.

As Dundee walks off toward the bullpen door, I call his name. "Coach. Thank you."

He steps back to me, tilting his head to give me an appraising look. "The way you do that is to be on this team next year."

"Yes, sir." That's why he rode my ass so much when I screwed up. Those few innings weren't what he was worried about, it was my career as a whole.

Warm-ups come and go, and when the game begins, I park my ass on the bench. All I think about is Avery straddling me on it. Maybe that's the secret. I need her in every part of this damn place to replace the old memories with new ones.

———

I'm just about to leave the stadium, lingering longer than normal in hopes of outlasting any persistent reporters waiting to get their shot at me. The coast is clear, though, even on the public side of the fence as I make my way to my truck and hop in the driver's seat.

My phone rings, the screen lighting up to show E.J. calling. Avery's student doesn't call often, but when he does, it's a nice relief and usually entertaining to chat with him.

Only today, he doesn't sound like his usual self as he asks, "Do you remember when you said I could call you if I ever needed anything?"

"Yep. Whatcha got?" I attempt to sound casual, but dread fills me as I predict this has something to do with the concern I saw on Avery's face as she'd watched her sleeping student in her classroom. The same look that prompted me to give E.J. my number to begin with.

"I need a lawyer."

"A lawyer? I'm going to need you to elaborate a bit more on that."

"I'll pay you back. I almost have all the money; I just can't wait any longer."

"E.J., it's not about the money. I'll pay whatever, but I need to know why you need one."

"I need to be emancipated."

I fear the answer but ask anyway. "Why?"

"Because my dad is a punk-ass bitch too."

That's how he saw through the Cash Barlowe Show. He knows a monster just like him. "Are you safe? Did something happen?"

"Nothing new. I'm good now. He's passed out." There're a few seconds of silence. "He went after my little brother. I can take care of myself, he can't."

Every muscle in my body constricts as my fingers squeeze the steering wheel. "Tell me your address." I crank up my truck's ignition and drive out to the edge of the parking lot.

"It'll make it worse. He's drunk and passed out and won't remember a thing in the morning. He'll think he fell or something. I just need to figure out how to get out of here permanently … and I need to bring my brother with me."

"How old is he?"

"Twelve."

"And your mother? Is she there?"

"No. My mother died seven years ago. It's just me and my brother. You can't tell anyone. They'll take Patrick and put him in a foster home. I promised him I wouldn't let that happen. If I'm on my own, and they can see that I'm capable, he can come with me."

The words twist at my chest as I picture the two young boys there with a carbon copy of my father. "E.J., it's not that simple."

"I know. But you know how this feels. I don't need simple. I need the fuck out of this house, and I need my brother with me."

"I'll see what our options are. But I need you to call me if something else happens. If he tries anything, get out of there and call me." It doesn't feel like enough. I want to get both of them someplace safe *now*.

"I will."

We chat for a few minutes and even after I hang up, I can't shake the feeling that I need to go get them right now. Once I'm at Avery's apartment, I walk inside to find her tucked comfortably on the sofa, watching TV. Her smile fades when she spots my expression. "What's wrong?"

I step to the sofa, dropping down as she sits straight up, her eyes not leaving me.

"E.J. just called me."

Her small gasp tells me she knows it wasn't good news.

"The reason he knew about my dad was because he's dealing with the same. He wants to get emancipated and take care of his twelve-year-old brother."

"Where are they? Are they safe?" She picks up her phone, clicking around before looking back to me.

"He asked me not to say anything, but they're still at

home. My lawyer is already working on it." But he didn't have any more confidence in the legal system working quickly than I did.

"I have to report it," she says looking back to her phone.

"I promised him."

Her fingers halt immediately as she looks up to me. "Carter, I'm legally mandated to report suspected abuse, and even if I wasn't required to, it *should* be reported."

"He promised his little brother he wouldn't go into foster care. Give my lawyers some time to see what options we have," I plead. Those troubled hazel eyes tell me she's having a real hard time going against her instinct. "Just give me until tomorrow."

She reluctantly agrees as we remain silent, only the sounds of the TV filling the apartment. After a few minutes, she moves closer, resting her head on my chest as my head falls back on the sofa. I know we need to report it, but I can't let them be separated from each other. I thought being lonely as a child was the worst thing ever, but I imagine having someone only to have them ripped away would be far worse.

42

CARTER

"I'll see you there." I kiss Avery, heading to the door. It's great knowing she'll be there, but I still feel a heavy cloud hanging overhead.

Once in my truck, I grab my phone and send off a quick message.

Me: You good?

E.J.: Yeah.

Me: I'm working on it, but it might take some time. We need to tell someone and get y'all out of there.

E.J: Like you told everyone about your dad?

Damn. That one hurts because it's the genuine truth.

Me: I should've told someone, but I didn't. And the ones who knew allowed it to continue. I can't be that person.

E.J.: I can't lose my brother.

Me: You won't. I promise you that.

Because I will do everything in my power to make sure he doesn't.

The drive to the stadium is quiet, and I see several news vans set up in the media spots outside the stadium. Of course, even without the added abuse story, today is a news day because it's my first game back since being suspended, and rumors still swirl that I might've injured my hand. I hadn't. I know it's fine, but I'm not issuing a goddamn statement about it. This time when I step on the field, it's not my arm I'm worried about cooperating. It's my mind.

My nerves at this game are getting to me. But once I see her smiling face sitting behind the dugout, most of it subsides. There's still a little bit that nags, but overall, I feel like I have a grip. I'll find out soon enough if my mental game is on lock when it's time to step up to the mound.

Once I'm there, I take a quick second to find her in the crowd. Her smile reaches her eyes as she stands on her feet, clapping and cheering with the rest of the crowd, Bodie beside her, cheering with his hands cupped around his mouth.

The first batter is an easy out, three strikes and done. The second gives me more of a challenge by tipping three balls foul but eventually strikes out. The third hitter pops a fly ball to right field that is caught. Three and done. Now I need to do it again. It's like riding a bike.

As I'm walking to the dugout, I look up to see hazel eyes peeking at me over the top of a book. I can't help but laugh and shake my head. Even though I can't see her mouth, I know she's smiling and teasing me because her eyes are twinkling with a playful glint. Damn, I never want those eyes to leave me.

Dropping onto the bench, I watch Dundee approach. A stiff posture to his body tells me he's not happy about something, and I know it's not my pitching. "He's here. I tried, but I was overruled."

Standing up, I walk to the edge of the dugout, and I know

exactly where he's going to be. Right behind home plate. It took some big balls for him to walk into the stadium with all the news that's going around. Maybe he thinks he can spin the story. Only, I don't give a fuck what he thinks. I know the story, and I know what I want to write for my future.

"I need a marker."

Dundee gives me a confused look as I pull my hat off my head, flipping my dad's old baseball card with *For me, not him* written on it. Coach steps away and returns in a few seconds, Sharpie in hand. I pop the cap off, make the adjustment, then hand the marker back to my very concerned-looking coach.

"I'm good. And if I'm not, I will be." I flash the card to him, then tuck it back in my hat and replace it on my head. Taking a seat until it's time for me to go out there again. Once on the field, I remove my hat, read the words then proceed with my game, not paying any mind to the man doing his best to distract me. Why? Because Avery nailed it. Cash knows I'm better than him, straight-up. The only way to convince himself he's better, is to fuck up my game. And that is powerful motivation. I didn't fight against him when I was a kid. But that's what I'll do now. I'll fight against the memories here, make my own in this stadium. *My* stadium.

Everything goes great, but Dundee pulls me after the fifth inning even though I don't get any runs scored off me. I don't complain or ask about my pitch count, though. He has my long game in mind, so I'll follow his lead because I trust him.

The Coyotes clinch the win, and the postgame interviewer eagerly looks my way. I know he's questioning if I'm going to bail. I'm not. Walking over to him, I spot Avery giving me a concerned look, though she's able to maintain a slight smile. I love that she's worried about me, but there's no need to be. Her waiting for me when all this is over is all I need to get through it. Because she sees the real me. There's no need for me to pretend anymore.

But I still brace myself. I know what's coming. And the reporter doesn't beat around the bush. "Great game back after that rough ejection two weeks ago. It must feel tremendous to be back, but how are you staying focused with all the attention surrounding the allegations of your father's abuse?"

Taking a deep breath, I look into the camera. "There has been a lot of attention focused on things that happened to me at the hand of my father off the field. And the allegations are true. But I'm on this field to do what I love. It's never been about him or his legacy. It's about waking up and doing what I love every day of my life … and doing it with the person I love by my side."

I glance over, seeing Avery's face, she's heard my words. Not exactly the way I'd planned to tell her I'd fallen in love with her, but I need it out in the open. She had to have known, but if not, she does now.

The reporter moves back to game-related questions and doesn't veer off topic to the beast I see standing on the edge of the field, speaking to the team manager. My father has the look I know well. He's pissed but trying to maintain his cool as he speaks to the coach.

Dundee walks over to me, slapping me on the shoulder as he walks by. "Don't be late for warm-ups tomorrow."

"You got it, Coach."

He halts, turning to look at me. "I'm proud of you, kid."

I smile and nod at him. I may just be a pitcher who's a pain in his ass, but he's given me exactly what my dad never did: A love and respect for the sport and myself. I can always depend on real talk and tough love from someone who wants me to succeed. I hadn't realized until he called me it, but I have come to feel like his kid, and damn, that's a good feeling.

I approach where a small crowd has gathered. I sign jerseys and some items that are handed to me. Most just say thanks and request a selfie, but I always engage with them. A few ask about baseball. A few tell me I had a great game and this is our year to go all the way. And to my absolute delight, not a single one mentions Cash Barlowe. In my periphery, I see him eventually walk off the field in a huff while I remain steadfast on my turf.

I slowly make my way over to the end of the line of fans, my favorite one waiting with a book in hand, Bodie beside her. I wrap my arms around her as she leans forward, the half-wall getting in the way, so I pick her up, bringing her feet to set on the dirt of the warning track.

"You did so great," she says against my lips as they cover hers.

"I hope you heard that interview and didn't fall asleep on me again."

She grins. "I heard it and feel the same, but I don't really want to tell the reporter that. I would like to know what you wrote on the baseball card."

"You saw that, huh?"

"Everyone saw that." She points to the jumbotron. "You looked determined."

"I was." Pulling my hat off, I pass her the card, and her expression changes as soon as she sees the word I marked out and the one I added as I repeat the sentiments aloud. "For us, not him. So, give me a few minutes because we have somewhere to be."

"Where's that?"

"E.J. and Patrick. We can't leave them to suffer behind closed doors in silence any longer. I've finally realized not telling the story is harder. We're gonna get them boys out of there."

She stands on her tiptoes, placing a quick kiss on my cheek. "I asked Joe for an update during the game, and he said the lawyers are making headway. So chop, chop."

"Joe? You're talking to my agent now?"

"I didn't have much of a choice. He called to lecture me about the importance of 'image.' Said I should be wearing a Coyotes jersey to support my man, even if it's not yours."

"Remind me to fire him later because there's no way in hell you're wearing anyone's number but mine."

"Whatever. You won't fire Joe. He knows it and I know it. Besides, you'll simmer down after a good blow."

"Hell yeah I will."

EPILOGUE

AVERY

Four months later

"You should've thrown the slider. Tried to tell you, but no. Mr. Baseball didn't listen." E.J. shakes his head with disappointment as Carter sits across the island, shoveling a scoop of scrambled eggs into his mouth.

"We didn't lose because of one pitch, E.J."

"Never know." E.J. lets his good-natured smile shine through as he's done messing with Carter about game five of the division series that they lost, ending their playoff bid. But the best part is the more the media picked up the story of the real Cash Barlowe, the more he faded off into the background. It's something I never saw coming, although I still keep my guard up, watching for him, and I know Carter does too. But I have no doubt if he shows, we'll both be ready to face him.

"It's okay. There's always next year." I attempt to reassure them all because as much as E.J. gives Carter a hard time about the loss, it hit him hard too.

"Eh. It's just a game. The important thing is what I do off

the field." Carter says it with sincerity and determination, but I know he wanted that title bad. "But we'll win next year."

"Yep!" E.J. and Patrick yell in unison as the three of them take turns high-fiving.

"Y'all need to hurry. We have to head out in a few minutes."

"Finally," E.J. mumbles, hurrying to the sink to clean his plate and place it in the dishwasher.

"Hey, bud. Really quick," Carter gives me an uneasy look before turning to E.J. "The emancipation isn't gonna go through today."

"Figures," he says, his head dropping a bit. "What happened?"

"I canceled it," Carter says simply.

E.J. looks between him and me as Patrick steps beside him, just enough to hide his face but enough to keep an eye on what's going on. We learned early on that it was the stance they'd take in front of their father, and it's still a second nature response that neither probably think much of. But it utterly breaks my heart.

"It's okay." Carter lightens his tone, obviously sensing that his seemingly good announcement has gone downhill fast. "We canceled because we want to adopt the both of you instead. If that's cool with y'all."

Patrick jumps out from behind E.J., running to Carter as he wraps his arms around his neck.

E.J. remains in place, a weary expression on his face as he looks between Carter and me. "Why?"

I step close to my former student who has become so much more in the last four months since he's arrived at the home with us. "Because we want you here, the both of you. Soon enough you'll be grown and on your own. We're not ready to send you off into the world yet, though, and you deserve some time to be a child before that day arrives."

His arms move around my waist as he clings to me. "Can I still change my name, please?"

"Sure. But can I ask what's so bad about Ernest?"

His eyes drop to his feet. "It's my dad's name."

"Whether you change it or keep it, it doesn't alter the fact that he has nothing to do with what's in here." Carter lightly taps a finger over E.J.'s heart. "But it's your decision."

"E.J. Barlowe ... that's what I want."

"Me too." Patrick chimes in. "But not E.J., just Patrick."

Carter chuckles, leaning down to whisper something in his ear before nodding to E.J. whose grin spreads across his face as he turns to look at me.

"What are y'all up to?" I know that look.

"Nothing." Carter steps in front of me as Patrick takes off out of the kitchen.

"Yeah, okay." I roll my eyes, knowing how my sister feels when the boys plot against her.

A few seconds later, Patrick enters and hands one of my paperback books to Carter. He passes it to me as I give him a curious look. Immediately, I recognize the worn cover of the very book I was reading that day at the field when we first met. It's not that hard for me to remember which story my mind was lost in that afternoon because I've been wrapped up in him since. But how does he remember? Examining the paperback, I see a little opening like something is stuck in it. As I open it, my hands freeze when I spot the gold band with a princess-cut solitaire diamond tucked between the pages.

"I was hoping we could have one more name change around here." He picks up the ring, dropping to one knee as he holds it up. "Marry me, Avery."

Speechless. There're no words. All I can do is stare at it and back to him several times before he lets out a nervous chuckle when I wrap my arms around his neck, holding on as tight as I can as he stands.

"Is that a yes?"

"Yes!"

He slides the ring on my finger, placing a soft kiss over it.

Damn, that book really does have a good ending.

ACKNOWLEDGMENTS

A big thank you to Kaitlyn and Jackson for the pregame talk that sparked the idea for this story.

To the real-life Dundee, a very big thank you! Your *coaching* on everything baseball is greatly appreciated!

Last but certainly not least … to Krista, where do I even begin? Editor just doesn't quite cover it. More like miracle-working, irreplaceable badass. Thank you so much for EVERYTHING! I seriously hit it out of the park when I found you.

ALSO BY ANDREA ROUSSE

ABOUT THE AUTHOR

Andrea is a native Louisianan from the mouth of the mighty Mississippi currently living out her happily-ever-after in Texas with her husband and two children.

Connect with Andrea:
www.andrearousse.com
Newsletter Signup

facebook.com/roussewrites
instagram.com/roussewrites
amazon.com/author/andrearousse

Made in United States
Orlando, FL
10 August 2022

20815567R00125